SPHERE OF POWER

Sphere of Power

Chronicles of the Chosen, Book 1

SHANON L. MAYER

Shanon Mayer

Copyright © 2021 by Shanon L. Mayer

All rights reserved. No part of this book may be reproduced in any manner whatsoever without written permission except in the case of brief quotations embodied in critical articles and reviews.

First Printing, 2021

~ 1 ~

MORGAN

After seven hours that felt like seven months on the road, the large burnt yellow moving truck turned off the highway and onto a smaller street. Morgan Lafayette leaned her head against the side window and looked out from the back seat of the truck's cab, watching the buildings crawl by as they drove past.

First was an old, run-down gas station with cigarette and beer ads plastered all over the walls and windows. After that came a restaurant with a large sign out front, announcing its dinner specials; apparently tonight was chicken fried steak night. Grocery stores, small clothing boutiques, a movie theater, and countless other stores followed. Morgan sighed and slumped back into her seat.

"I still don't see why we have to move all the way out here," she grumbled. "We don't even know anybody."

Susan Lafayette, Morgan's mother, looked up into the rearview mirror and met Morgan's eyes. Her eyes were surrounded with her customary bright eye makeup, today it was light purple. "You know why we had to move. Your father needed a new job and this was the best he was able to get. So we'll have to make the best of it, even if is a long way from home. We have a nicer house now, not just a little apartment; you'll have a nice back yard to play in, too."

"A back yard?" Morgan looked doubtfully at her mother. "I'm not a kid anymore. I don't just go out to play in the yard." Morgan would be turning thirteen in four more days and didn't like being thought of as a child.

"I know that but it'll be a nice place to have a picnic, or a barbecue, or have all of your new friends over for your birthday party."

Morgan snorted. "As if I'm going to have a

lot of friends by this weekend. I didn't even have that many friends back home, and I was there for *years*." She looked out the window again, sulking, as her mother turned her attention back to the road.

Not seeing much to hold her interest outside the cab of the truck, she looked instead at her own reflection. Her hair hung to just past her shoulders in a tangled, curly mess. It didn't matter how many bottles of hair spray, styling gel, and mousse her mother bought for her, it never looked any different, and refused to do anything but tangle up behind her Fifteen minutes after she dragged a comb through it in the morning, it looked as though she had slept on it all over again.

She picked up a strand of the hair and examined the ends, wondering what she would look like with a different color than the light brown she had. Blond would be nice but she didn't want to endure the "dumb blond" jokes that would surely follow. Maybe a darker shade of brown would be better.

Her eyes were a much darker brown, almost the color of her father's morning coffee before he added the cream to it. The rest of her face was just a face, with a nose about the right size and shape, in her own opinion. It was turned slightly up at the tip and during the heat of summer there would be a smattering of freckles across it and invading onto her cheeks – yet another thing she wasn't looking forward to.

She had her mother's chin, kind of thin and pointed, which she thought made her face look like an almond standing on its tip. Although her mother always fussed over her, trying to get her to wear dresses because she would be "such a pretty girl," she didn't see the point in it. Tomboy or princess, she was just plain boring Morgan anyway, so she just wore what she was comfortable in. Today, as usual, she was dressed in baggy jeans and a long-sleeved tee shirt, with her old, worn-out sneakers that her mother kept threatening to throw away. She was short for her age, so her jeans were always frayed at the bottoms where they dragged on the ground.

Finally, they turned off of the main street into a residential area and Morgan started looking for her father's car. David Lafayette had traveled up ahead of them to finalize the purchase of the house and get settled into his new job, so Morgan and her mother hadn't seen him in over a week. As they drove past house after house, Morgan saw no sign of her father's little silver Honda.

They turned onto another side street and it looked like they were leaving town again already. The houses were further apart and the road was a lot worse. Instead of smooth pavement, this street was badly cracked and chipped, with more gravel than whole blacktop. At the very end of the road, they turned down a gravel driveway and Morgan saw her father's car. In dismay, she looked up at the house, hoping that they were in the wrong place.

It was two stories tall, without a lot of windows, and the paint had long since faded to a dull grey. Morgan could see the edge of a chimney off to the side of the house, grayish stones hunched against the wall as though they were trying to hide from view. The porch sagged to the side and one of the steps was missing completely. It had a yard, just as her mother had promised, with grass and weeds that were as tall as Morgan's waist. As she climbed out of the truck, Morgan squinted to see inside the windows, hoping it wouldn't be as bad inside as it looked like from the outside. At least none of the windows were broken.

Her father walked out the front door soon after they parked and waved at them, grinning broadly under his slightly graying mustache that looked like the business end of a broom. He was dressed, as always, in a dark grey suit and red tie, with highly polished black shoes. Morgan had seen a couple of her dad's coworkers from the bank he had worked at before the move and it seemed that this type of suit was the uniform for a loan officer. "You found it!"

He led them inside and gave them a tour of the house, through the kitchen, living, dining and laundry rooms downstairs. Upstairs, he showed them the bedrooms, and Morgan discovered that not only was her room almost twice the size of her old room, now she would have her own bathroom as well. No more having to wait for her father to finish his hour-and-a half shower after work and no more having to wait for her mother to finish getting primped in the morning before she could even brush her teeth.

The rest of the day was spent trying to get as much unloaded from the truck and brought into the house as possible. Once all of Morgan's boxes and furniture had been brought upstairs to her room, she was left alone to unpack. She shoved her bed against a wall and pushed her desk over next to the window, then dragged her dresser over next to the door. She had always liked having a bit of space in the middle of her room to stretch out in. Plus, this way she could sit at her desk and draw whatever she saw out there, even if there wasn't a whole lot to be seen. As she opened the first box of clothes, she heard a strange scratching sound coming from behind her.

She turned around to look but didn't see anything. It sounded like the noise was coming from under her bed, so she cautiously walked over to it, knelt on the floor, and peeked beneath. There was nothing under there, but the noise stopped.

She looked around for the source of the noise for a few minutes before dismissing it and putting her clothes away. Once her dresser was full, she picked up an armful of clothes and headed for her closet. Halfway there, she heard the scratching noise again, as if something was climbing inside her walls.

She dropped the clothes and ran downstairs to look for her parents. They were in the kitchen, putting dishes into the cupboards. "There's something in my room."

Her parents followed her up to her room, where she pointed to the closet. "It started under the bed, but then it moved into there."

Her dad opened the closet and looked inside. "There's nothing there," he told her. "It was probably just the house settling. Old houses like this make noises sometimes but it's nothing to be afraid of."

Her mother helped her pick the clothes off the floor as her father headed back downstairs. "New places can be kind of scary, I know, but you will feel better once you have a good night's sleep. Now put these away and get ready for bed. You start school tomorrow."

In the morning, Morgan's father dropped her off at a large building made out of a pattern of red and brown bricks. It was only one story tall, shorter than her last school had been, with a large awning over the front entrance and an enormous blue dolphin painted on the wall of an entryway that was crammed with people.

"Great, I get to be a Denver Heights Dolphin this year," she muttered to herself. On the side of the school, she could see a baseball field and more sports areas beyond it.

Before she climbed out of the car, her father handed her a piece of paper with her classroom number, teacher's name, and other important information on it. "Give this to your teacher, and he will handle the rest of it."

Morgan looked over the paper. She would be in room fifteen, and her teacher's name was Mr. Evans. She nodded and climbed wordlessly out of the car. She hefted her backpack onto her shoulder and walked up the sidewalk into the brick school.

Inside, the halls were packed with people, both students and teachers. Morgan threaded her way through the crowd, trying to keep track of the numbers on the doors to find her classroom. Students ran past, shoving and pushing, with teachers yelling at them to slow down. Once, Morgan was knocked to the ground, and she had to move quickly to not be trampled. Finally, she found room number fifteen, and gratefully slipped inside.

A man, who she assumed was Mr. Evans, stood at the front of the classroom. He was dressed in tan-colored pants and a dark brown shirt with buttons down the front. As Morgan watched, he picked up some chalk and began writing the states and their capital cities on the chalkboard. Only a few students were in the room, but more were filing in behind Morgan. She walked up to the teacher and held out the paper.

"Ah, you must be Morgan Lafayette." He took the paper and smiled at her. "We've been expecting you." He looked around at the class, which was quickly filling up, and pointed towards a desk along the left side of the classroom, next to the windows. "I believe that seat is vacant, why don't you sit there?"

Morgan nodded and headed towards the desk, fully aware that all of the students in the class were staring at her. She dropped her backpack onto the floor next to the desk and slid into the seat, wishing she could just disappear, or better yet, return to her old school.

Class in her new school was pretty much the same as class had been in her old school. The teachers talked for hours about the same things while the students whispered, giggled, and tried not to get caught passing notes to each other. When she realized that they were learning about the state capitals, she barely stifled a groan; she had just finished covering that in her last school.

Mr. Evans was a lot more amusing than her last teacher had been, with an interesting fact about each of the capitals that they talked about. To Morgan's surprise, he even managed to make her laugh a couple of times as he changed his accent to some of the areas that they talked about. When they talked about New York, he sounded like sound like Joe Pesci. When they talked about Alabama, he sounded like Jeff Foxworthy. What really got her laughing was California, where he gave an absolutely horrible impersonation of Swarzenegger. Even so, Morgan was relieved to hear the final bell ring so that she could go home and be away from it all. She stuffed all of her papers into her backpack and headed outside, looking at the line of cars full of parents waiting for their children.

She wasn't surprised when her mother wasn't there to pick her up. Susan Lafayette was always busy with one thing or another and tended to lose track of time, so Morgan walked home more often than not. Today, she just hoped that she would be able to remember where she lived. She headed off campus and into the neighborhood, looking for anything that looked familiar. She thought she remembered the little yellow house with the white trim but she couldn't remember if she was supposed to turn there or keep going straight. After only a couple of wrong turns, she finally found her house.

As she had expected, her mother was home, typing on the computer, talking on the phone, taking notes with a notepad, pen, and switching through news channels on the television. She was a patent reviewer, so she was always researching to see if there were existing patents for things that people invented. Morgan had no idea what her mother was actually doing most of the time but she was always busy and always doing more things at the same time than should have been humanly possible. Morgan left her to whatever she was doing and went upstairs.

At her desk, she dropped her backpack onto the floor and started her math assignment, wondering what the point of it all was. She had already done all this just a couple of months ago and resented having to do it again. She didn't get too far into her homework before becoming bored, so she pulled out a fresh piece of paper and began doodling.

The drawings weren't much at first, just a few strange-looking shapes but soon she started to turn the shapes into figures and before long she had a paper full of croaking and jumping frogs. She added some lily pads and water, quickly hiding the sketch in a drawer when she heard footsteps on the stairs. When her mother peeked in the door, she was hard at work on her math homework.

That night, after Morgan went to bed, she was jolted awake by the scratching noises again.

These noises sounded a lot louder than the ones before, so her eyes flew open and she looked around but wasn't able to see anything that could have caused the sounds. She scanned the shadowed areas more fully than the areas that had light shining in from the window but couldn't spot anything suspicious. After what felt like hours but was probably just a matter of minutes, the sounds finally faded and she relaxed.

When the sounds started again, however, she got out of bed and padded down to her parents' room. Knocking softly on their door, she opened it a crack and peeked in. "There's a noise in my room again."

David, her father, groaned and rolled out of bed. "It's probably nothing, Morgan." He walked to her room and turned on the light. "Where did you hear the noise?"

Morgan pointed to the corner where she thought the sounds had come from and watched as her father looked for anything that could have made the noises. "There's nothing here." He turned back to her. "Go back to bed." He tucked her back into her bed and left the door slightly open when he walked out of the room.

Morgan barely slept that night. Every sound inside the house, from the creaking of the floorboards down the hall to the scratching sounds on the glass from the trees outside, woke her again. She could clearly hear the ticking of the huge clock that stood in the hallway downstairs. She couldn't hear it during the day but at night it sounded as though it was posted directly outside her door. Worse, sometimes it sounded like the ticking sounds were getting closer and closer, as though the clock was moving towards her room, either being carried by some monster or, worse yet, having grown legs of its own so that it could pursue her itself. She reminded herself that it was the same clock it had always been, both in this house and the one they had lived in before, and it wasn't dangerous.

When morning came and light began to brighten the room, she was finally able to fall asleep. All too soon, it was time to get up for school.

When she went downstairs for breakfast, her

mother put a plate of pancakes on the table in front of her. "Have you decided who to invite to your party this weekend?"

Morgan poured syrup across the plate and shook her head. "It's only been a couple of days; I don't exactly have a lot of friends here yet."

"That's okay," her mother responded. "We can have a party with just family, that'll be fun too. What about presents? Have you decided what you want yet?"

Morgan took a bite of the pancakes and tried not to grimace. For all that her mom did, she had never quite managed to make pancakes without crunchy bits in them. "Dad said you were getting me more clothes."

"Well, yes, we're getting you more clothes, but I thought you might want something fun, too."

"I suppose moving home isn't an option, is it?" When her mother just shook her head, Morgan thought it over. "I was thinking that a new video game console would be cool, but there are a few new games that I would like to have, too."

"A console might be a little bit too expensive right now, but I think we can manage a couple of games." Her mom smiled down at her. "You excited yet?"

"Not really." Morgan poked at the stack of pancakes again, debating whether to risk another bite. "It's not like anything's going to change, is it?"

Her mother sighed. "Your father has to leave early for work, so if you want a ride in to school, you need to hurry up and finish your breakfast."

Thankful for the excuse, Morgan pushed her plate away. "I'm not really that hungry today." She stood up and headed for the stairs. "I just need my backpack and I'll meet him out at the car."

When she walked into her room, Morgan had the unmistakable feeling of being watched. She looked around apprehensively as she picked up her backpack, but didn't see what could have been causing the feeling. She hitched the bag up onto her shoulder and left the room, fairly running down the stairs on her way out of the house. She didn't say anything on the ride to school; she just stared out the window and watched as the town cruised past.

Morgan wasn't really paying that much attention in class. While Mr. Evans explained to the class about the first settlers in North America, she was busily staring out the window. A monarch butterfly with enormous yellow and black wings had landed on the windowsill just beyond the glass and Morgan wanted to draw it before it flew away again. She wished, not for the first time, that she had some colored pencils. Even then, she wasn't positive that colored pencils would really show how golden the butterfly's wings really were.

Just as she started to add some surrounding features so that the grey-and-black butterfly on the paper wasn't just floating in a sea of white, she noticed that Mr. Evans was starting to circle the class. She covered the drawing with a page that had various different notes on it and pretended that she had been paying attention the whole time. When Mr. Evans dropped the pop quiz onto her desk in front of her, Morgan dropped her head onto her desk.

Walking home from school, Morgan noticed a butterfly that looked a lot like the one that she had drawn in class. It fluttered around her, not appearing to head in any particular direction but staying close enough that Morgan could watch it. As she turned down the road that led to her house, however, the butterfly darted off. Morgan watched it as it faded into the distance before heading inside.

The feeling of being watched and the scratching sounds continued for the next number of weeks. After the first couple of days, Morgan stopped going to her parents every time she heard a noise; they never really seemed to take her concerns seriously. Instead, she tried to ignore them because whatever was watching her and following her around during the day didn't seem to be harmful.

Morgan turned her bed so that it faced away from the window, tired of watching strange shadows flicker across the glass during the night. She moved her CD player over to the desk and plugged headphones into it so that she couldn't hear the sounds while she worked on her homework. Whenever she felt something watching her, she couldn't help herself from looking around, but otherwise tried to ignore it.

That weekend, Morgan's parents brought

home a cake from the grocery store, frosted white with colorful balloons all over it and bright blue lettering that spelled, "Happy Birthday Morgan!" After an early dinner of pizza and Pepsi, they brought out more gifts than Morgan had expected. As usual, she got a few new dresses because her mother kept trying to insist that she needed to dress like a girl. Thankfully, the dresses weren't all the clothes she received; she also got a couple new pairs of jeans and a teal-blue hooded sweater.

To her surprise, the last gift she unwrapped was the gaming console she had asked for. There were a couple of games with it too: Call of Duty, Guitar Hero, and one of those obnoxious dancing games that had to have been her mother's idea.

After about a month, the noises and sensation of being watched were no longer confined to her bedroom. She felt it downstairs while she was eating breakfast, she felt it while she was at school pretending to be paying attention, and she even felt it while she was out and about in town.

She stopped in the grocery store once while

she was out shopping with her mother because she thought she heard someone whispering her name. She immediately turned around to look, but nobody was there. Not that she had expected there to be.

Not for the first time, Morgan wondered if this was what it felt like to be going crazy.

The strange scratching sounds woke her night after night. Her parents still insisted that the noises were just the sounds of the old house settling but Morgan's eyes snapped wide open each time a new noise sounded. She rolled over onto her side and tried to remind herself that the scratching sounds she could hear in between the ticking of the clock were just branches of the bushes outside her room scratching against the wall and the windows in response to the wind. The shadows she could see drifting across her windows behind the pretty curtains her mother had put up were just the branches, not monsters trying to find a way in from outside.

Except she didn't believe it.

She could hear the wind, too. It moaned and groaned, complaining almost as much as the house did. Morgan could hear it howl through the bushes and sigh down into the chimney like a lonely, miserable ghost.

She rolled over onto her other side and took a few deep breaths, reminding herself that there was nothing to be afraid of; it was all the same stuff that she had been scared of every night and she had never been able to find out what was causing them. Whatever it was had never actually tried to hurt her, she tried to reason with herself, so it probably wasn't that dangerous.

"Yeah, right," she muttered out loud, not believing her own reasoning in the slightest.

~ 2 ~

TILSON

She had almost settled herself to sleep once again when a new type of scratching jolted her back awake. This wasn't the arrhythmic rubbing of the bushes but a steadier, secretive noise, less of a scratching noise and more a sound of something trying *not* to scratch as it moved. What was worse, as she listened to it, was that she could hear whatever was causing it enter her room. She could hear something as it crossed the floor of her bedroom, and the noises stopped at about the point where whatever it was reached the small area rug that her mother had put in front of the bed.

Whatever was causing that noise was *right next to her!*

Morgan froze. She held as still as she could, barely even breathing and listening to her pulse roar in her ears. After a countless number of heartbeats, she decided that whatever it was in her room, she didn't want it sneaking up on her; she wanted to be aware of where it was.

Since she could no longer hear it, she opened her eyes, just barely, which was more than enough to see a pair of dark brown eyes in a tiny face with a nose that was much too large peering back at her.

She squeezed her eyes closed once more, positive that when she opened them again, whatever it was would be gone. She had thought her heart was racing just hearing the noises; that was nothing compared to now. She held her breath, trying desperately to believe that there really hadn't been anything there. When she opened her eyes again, she knew, she would realize that all she had seen was a shadow, her imagination, a fragment of a dream, *something*. There really hadn't been a tiny little man, standing on her pillow and staring at her as she slept. Of course there wasn't. There couldn't have been.

She opened one eye, ever so slightly, slowly enough that if there was something there, maybe it wouldn't notice that little bit of movement. Which was silly, because there would be nothing there, she was sure.

It was still there, looking at her, its fuzzy, pointed ears slightly cocked, as if it was listening to her breathing. Listening for something it couldn't possibly be hearing, because Morgan was still holding her breath.

Trying not to scream for her parents, Morgan scooted back away from the creature and sat bolt upright. She gasped as she moved, her choked breath catching in her throat. As she backed away, the creature rolled backwards a short distance, almost falling off the bed. It caught itself with an edge of the pillowcase and began to pull itself back up where it could stand again.

Morgan scooted back away from the strange creature and pulled the covers tighter against her chest. She watched as it climbed from the pillowcase to the sheet over her and stood up again, its feet spread a bit further for balance. When she had a little more control over her vocal cords, Morgan whispered, "What are you?"

"And a fine greeting that was too, almost knocking me to the floor like that. One would think that you were a much ruder little girl." Its voice was high and a bit shrill, fitting for the size of the body that it was coming from.

Morgan blinked in surprise. Now that she had a better look at the small creature, looking at it from more than an inch or two away, it didn't appear nearly as frightening as she had originally thought. It was shaped like a human, only a very small one. It stood only a few inches tall, half a foot at most. Light brown fur covered most of its body, including the long, mouse-like tail. Its tail had a puff of dark orange fur at the tip like a poodle in a cartoon and a matching pouf stuck straight up from the top of its head. It was dressed in what appeared to be scraps of cloth, stitched together to make rudimentary clothing.

"Sorry…I was surprised. Are you OK?"

The small creature brushed itself off and leaned its head back so that it could look Morgan in the eye. "Yes, yes, I am fine, I didn't fall, and you see...I caught myself. I am Tilson." As he spoke, the creature held out a tiny, fur-covered hand towards Morgan.

Morgan held out her hand as well, extending a finger for Tilson to shake. "But what are you?"

After shaking Morgan's finger, Tilson leaned closer and whispered, "I am a haltija."

"A what?" Morgan whispered back.

"A haltija. I live here, just like you do."

Morgan blinked. "But I haven't ever seen you before. Where have you been?"

"Of course you haven't seen us; no human can until we decide to be seen. And we try to stay hidden, because your people are dangerous to my people. Big, clumsy humans, always stepping on us."

"Then why can I see you now?"

"You can see me because I chose to make myself seen." He let go of her finger and considered his words. "Well, it wasn't much of a choice, really. I was told to contact you, so here I am, talking to you." He paced back and forth across her bedcovers as he spoke before stopping to look up at her again. "Why are you looking at me like that?"

Morgan gaped at the small creature and asked, dumbfounded, "Why were you told to contact me?"

"The council said that we needed help from a human and you were the closest human that fit the requirements. You see, we have been keeping an eye on you since you moved here and they finally decided that you would do, so they sent me here to make contact.

"The council thinks that I should be the one to work with you, at least for a while, until you figure out what you are doing. So here I am. You see," the haltija looked around to make sure that they were alone and that nobody else could overhear him before continuing. "We need your help."

Morgan leaned down closer, to better be able to hear Tilson, as his voice had dropped even more quiet than before. "Help with what?"

"With finding the dragons, of course. A lot of them have gone missing, and the council looked into it, and they think that there are humans involved. So...we decided to contact a human to help. So they sent me to you."

Morgan sat back again, stunned for the second time in less than half an hour. This really couldn't be happening. "Dragons? You mean *real* dragons?"

Tilson cocked an eyebrow at her. "Would I be here, talking with you, if they weren't real?"

"But...dragons? Aren't they big and scary and like to eat people?"

"Have you ever heard of someone actually being eaten by a dragon? That's just an ugly rumor that lots of people passed around a long time ago, trying to give dragons a bad name." He seemed to think about it for a couple of moments. "But you probably still don't want to upset any of them too much, just in case."

"But...I don't know anything about dragons. How could I possibly be able to find them?"

Tilson took a deep breath. Pointing at Morgan, he said "You are a human. Not a dragon, you are a human." He said it slowly, being careful to pronounce each word clearly. "We know that humans are involved, so you need to look for clues that a human would leave behind, not clues that a dragon would leave, because you are not a dragon, you are a human."

Morgan was starting to wonder why he kept repeating himself. Did he really think that she hadn't heard him? "But...wouldn't someone else be better to help you with that? I'm just a kid."

The haltija shook his head quickly, which caused his tail to swish back and forth a few times. "No, no, no. Look, you are what, thirteen, right?" When Morgan nodded, Tilson continued, "You see, when humans get much older than you are, they have a harder time believing in us: dragons, me, and all the rest of the other fey. You are as old as you can be to still be able to help us. If all this had happened only about a year later, I wouldn't be here talking to you at all, I would have been sent to find a different, younger, human."

"Fey?"

"Yes, fey. All of us who live in the hidden, magical world are called fey. You humans have your world and we have ours. The two worlds overlap, so we are able to travel back and forth a bit, but they are still separate. You are human, we are fey. Get it?"

"There's another world that's here with us?" Morgan thought about this and shook her head. "That's not possible, is it?"

"Of course it's possible. Not just possible, but it's real. That's why humans don't know about us and why you normally can't see us. We stay in our world for the most part and leave you to yours." He paced back and forth across her bed again as he explained. "But sometimes the council decides that we need to work with the humans, so one of us is sent over to find one that will work."

He stepped up onto her pillow and tapped one little foot. "Humans see things differently than we do. You might see something that we wouldn't. So you come with us to look around, find whatever is there that we haven't found, then we bring you back home. It's that easy."

"But how can there be two worlds here like that?"

"With magic, of course." The haltija stood up. "Now are you coming with me, or not?"

Morgan considered this for a moment and decided that it made about as much sense as anything else had on this crazy night. Maybe it was all just some weird dream that she would wake up from soon, so she might as well go along with it. This was already more of an adventure than she had ever been on and it looked like it was going to get a lot more exciting. "So how am I supposed to find these clues?"

"They will be in the dragon's lair. We just have to go there and look. It's that easy."

Morgan nodded, still trying to grasp what was going on. "Okay, so we have to go to the dragon's lair to look for these clues. How are we supposed to get there? I don't even know where a dragon lair would be."

Tilson grinned, and the sides of his mouth seemed to reach to either side of his face, further than any mouth that Morgan had ever seen before. "We fly, of course."

"You can fly?" Of all the things the haltija had told her so far, this was the most amazing. "How can you fly, when you don't even have wings?"

Tilson's grin faded as he sighed and spoke to Morgan in that slow, careful voice again. "I am a haltija. I don't have wings, so I can't fly. Understand?"

"But you said we were going to fly. I don't have wings either."

"Of course you don't have wings you are a human. Humans don't have wings."

Morgan nodded. "Right. So how are we going to get there?"

"We fly." When Morgan groaned, Tilson continued. "But first, you need to get dressed. You probably don't want to go out like that."

Morgan realized that she was still in her pajamas and she definitely didn't want to go out in the middle of the night hunting for clues in her nightgown. She climbed out from under the covers and headed for her dresser, not wanting to risk waking up her parents by turning on a light.

After putting on a sweater and a pair of jeans, she pulled on a pair of socks and stepped into her tennis shoes, feeling a bit disappointed. If this was all just a dream, she shouldn't have still been in her pajamas and her favorite sweater, the one she had gotten for her birthday only a month before, would at least be clean instead of sitting at the bottom of her laundry basket where she had put it the day before yesterday.

Well, she figured, since it was already dirty, wearing it again to go see a dragon's lair wouldn't hurt anything. She pulled it down over her head and rolled up the ends of the sleeves, which were still a little bit too long. Since it got pretty cold out at night, she put on her jacket as well, just in case. Tiptoeing across her room, she headed down the hall, down the stairs and stopped for a couple extra seconds in the kitchen. If she was going out on this crazy adventure, she was at least going to be prepared.

Even though she couldn't see him in the dark, she could feel Tilson tugging on her pant leg, urging her to head for the door, but she shushed the haltija and headed instead for the drawer where her parents always kept the emergency flashlight. She had seen enough scary movies to know better than to walk out of the house in the middle of the night without a flashlight; that was practically asking for horrible things to happen to you. After flashing it on and off a couple times to be sure that the batteries worked, she scooped up Tilson and snuck out the back door, pulling it quietly closed behind them.

The night air was crisp and cold, making Morgan happy that she had remembered her coat. The wind, mild as it was, soon warmed her cheeks, and she could see her breath fogging out before her. "So how're we supposed to fly to the lair?" She was starting to wonder if all of this really was a dream or not because she couldn't remember being this cold in a dream before. In her normal dreams, everything was just kind of warm and there wasn't usually any wind. She wrapped her arms tighter around herself and looked around, trying to see anything that would take Tilson and her to their destination. All she saw was the back yard with trees off to the south and a highway off in the distance.

Tilson crawled up her arm and perched on Morgan's shoulder, taking hold of one of her coat's lapels. "Askel will take us."

"Who is Askel?" Although they were outside and not as likely to wake her parents, Morgan kept her voice low. "Or should I ask what?"

Tilson leaned forward, keeping hold of the

lapel for balance, and pointed towards the grove of trees at the edge of the back yard. "That's Askel."

Morgan didn't see anything but trees at first, but as they got closer to the point where Tilson was indicating, she could see a shape, barely shimmering in the gloom. It looked like the heat rising from the street on a hot day, or the gas wafting up from the barbecue when her dad felt like cooking dinner in the back yard. As she got closer, the form solidified, becoming larger and more real.

At first, she thought it was a giant cat, almost the size of her father's car. Then she noticed that it had wings like those of a huge bird, kind of like an eagle, sprouting from its shoulders. Its feathers were brown, starting very dark towards the top and fading to a light tan color at the bottom. Its front legs ended in the claws of the same kind of huge bird. Morgan's walk slowed as she approached, and the beast turned to face her. Its head was birdlike as well, with creamy, ivory-colored feathers covering it down to the base of its neck and a sharp, dangerous looking dark brown beak. The rest of the creature's body was catlike, with golden brown fur from neck to tail, which was swishing back and forth behind it.

Again, Morgan found herself holding her breath. She slowed down, slightly afraid to approach the magnificent creature.

"Be nice now, Askel doesn't like rude people. Be polite and respect him, else he might drop us off before we get there."

Morgan barely heard Tilson's voice, close to her ear as he was. She was too busy looking along the length of Askel before slowly reaching out a hand to stroke the soft fur just below the feathers on his neck. His? Morgan couldn't be sure if this was a he or a she. How did one tell with a creature such as this? Tilson had referred to him as a he, so Morgan would just have to go with that. She buried her fingers in the soft fur, and ran her hand down over the strong shoulder, amazed at the feel. "Hello, Askel. I'm Morgan."

Askel didn't answer. Instead, he lowered himself so that his belly was almost on the ground, low enough that Morgan would be able to easily climb up onto his back.

Once Morgan was securely seated atop Askel, she looked down in front of her, where Tilson had placed himself. "Won't people see us if we are flying like this?"

Once again, Tilson gave her a look of incredulity, as though he couldn't understand why the girl was asking so many questions to which the answers should be obvious. "Well, have you ever seen a gryphon out flying around before? No, you haven't. That's because humans can't see us unless we choose to be seen." He settled in a bit more comfortably on Askel's back. "I think I may have mentioned that already."

Morgan leaned down closer to Askel's back. "Humans can see me, though, so that means that they won't see you and Askel, they'll just see me, flying all by myself. Won't that look a little strange?"

Tilson sighed again and leaned forward to grab hold of Askel's fur. "No, they won't see you, because you will be with us. So that means that we would all have to want to be seen for any of us to be seen." As Askel rose up to his feet and began to pace across the lawn towards the hillside further out, he continued, but in a much smaller voice. "Unless they are humans who are already familiar with us or someone from our world. Then, they will probably see us just fine."

"You mean there are people who know about you? People have seen you before? I thought you said that you guys stay hidden." Almost as soon as she asked, she thought about all of the stories she had heard about people who went crazy and started talking to things that weren't there. Maybe they weren't all so crazy after all.

Askel started to pick up speed, practically galloping by the time they reached the edge of the clearing. Just as the ground dropped below them, falling down the side of the hill, his great wings stretched out, rose straight into the air and the great beast leaped, thrusting his wings down as he took air. Morgan threw herself forward, expecting to be tossed off his back, but the flight started surprisingly gracefully. As Askel's wings beat up and down, slowly but steadily, his back under Morgan rocked gently back and forth and Morgan didn't even fall off like she had expected.

Even so, she leaned in tight to Askel, hoping that none of the people that Tilson had mentioned could see them would notice one small girl, clutching to the neck of the giant creature as they flew towards the distant mountains. At first, she had tufts of Askel's fur clutched tight in her fists but soon she began to relax and let go of the fur. She ran her hands along Askel's neck below the feathers, eventually moving her hands up to smooth the feathers along his neck as well.

Morgan was fairly certain after one brief glance over the side of Askel's back that she had never ridden this fast in her father's car before. She wasn't even certain that her father's car *could* go this fast, for that matter. The land beneath them moved past with terrifying speed, rivers, roads, and patches of houses, all blending together into one blur of color. Wind buffeted her as they moved through the clear night sky.

As they flew on, Morgan relaxed more and sat up straighter, much to Tilson's relief. "Thought you were going to squash me completely there. Weren't you listening when I was telling you that all your people are big clumsy oafs? Humans never seem to realize how big they are, or that they are heavy. That's why I said that. I can't breathe when you are lying across me like that." He stretched his back and took a deep breath. "Stop worrying, Askel's not going to drop you."

Despite Tilson's grumbling, Morgan grinned. This was the best ride of her life. She leaned back a bit more, rocking with the rhythm of Askel's wings and looked around her. She could see a formation of birds off to her left and a large passenger plane in the distance off to her right. She waved at the plane, wondering if any of the passengers could see her and what any of them would do if they could. She knew that planes, or maybe it was just at the airport, had radar, devices that let the pilots know if there was anything flying too close to the plane. She wondered if someone out there had noticed them through one of those, since the fey magic couldn't work on machines... could it? Soon, she stopped wondering about these things and just watched the world around her as they flew on and on.

Soon after, a series of mountains peaked on the horizon. As the small group got closer, Askel headed more directly towards a particular mountain, one that was quite a bit different than any other that Morgan had ever seen. To her knowledge, mountain tops were supposed to be relatively smooth and covered with either snow or trees and other vegetation, not broken, bulbous and charred as this one was. It looked as though a part of the top had blown completely open, scattering bits and pieces of mountain all over the surrounding area.

~ 3 ~

DRAGON'S LAIR

They landed on a softer portion of the mountain, avoiding most of the blackened, broken rocks and charred trees that surrounded them. As Morgan climbed down from Askel's back and helped Tilson down as well, she could see a small opening in the mountainside a short distance away.

"Is that the lair?" She pointed towards the opening as she spoke, so that the haltija would have no doubt as to what she was asking.

"I think so. Looks like it would be a dragon's lair, now doesn't it?"

"You mean you aren't sure?" Morgan looked down at Tilson incredulously.

"I haven't been here before either," he shrugged. "Besides, what else would it be?"

Morgan crept into the lair, turning on her flashlight so that she could see more clearly. Although she had expected it to be dark, somehow she hadn't expected the total blackness that filled the interior of the cave. The walls of the tunnel leading into the depths of the mountain were rough stone and looked as though they had been blasted apart by some huge explosion. Gouges and cracks ran along the opening of the lair, leading deeper inside. Very little dust had settled along the bottom of the tunnel and no spiders had spun their webs across it either. For that, Morgan was relieved. She didn't want to see what kind of spiders would live this close to a dragon.

Deeper inside, the tunnel opened into a wide, deep cavern. Standing at the entrance, Morgan shone her light into the depths but the chamber was so large that the beam was unable to reach the far wall. She walked along the edge of the room, looking along the walls and the floor close to the edge. More cracks, looking much like those at the entrance, crisscrossed the walls in here as well. Morgan ran her fingers along a section of gouging, noticing that there were places in the cracks where she could press her finger inside almost to the second knuckle.

Although Morgan had expected the air to be cooler in the interior of the cave, it seemed to her as though it was a little bit warmer. She paused for a moment to consider this but quickly dismissed it as imagination. Everyone knew that it wasn't warmer in the shade.

As she circled the chamber, she discovered a number of smaller tunnels, much like the one that led to the outside, leading off in all directions. She guessed that none of these tunnels led to the surface because she couldn't feel any sort of a breeze coming from any of them as she passed. Briefly, she considered exploring some of the tunnels but decided it would be best to finish her examination of the main cavern first.

Rubble was strewn about the main chamber, with a massive pile of rocks on one of the far reaches of the cavern wall. Morgan slowed down, taking care to not trip over any of the stones that were scattered and loose across the uneven floor. A couple of pebbles, jarred loose as she stepped across them, clattered across the floor, echoing through the enormous cave.

Suddenly, the mound of stones that Morgan had just played her light over moved, sending rocks and small pebbles tumbling across the floor in an explosive clatter. Tilson squeaked and dashed behind a large boulder. Morgan took a few hasty steps backwards and slipped on a patch of loose stones. With a thump, she landed on her backside in the middle of the cavern floor. Almost losing her flashlight as she fell, she tightened her grip on the handle and turned the beam to where the stones had fallen.

As one of the larger stones fell to the floor, a mass of tangled hair pushed through a narrow gap in the rocks. The hair was attached to a dirty, deeply lined head, which was in turn attached to the body of a short, stocky man. He stood just less than four feet tall and was nearly as wide. As he climbed out onto the floor of the cavern, the hole behind him filled in with loose stones, soon appearing as though there had never been any opening.

Morgan kept the light trained on the man, hoping that the glare would blind him, in case he decided to attack. Trying to move as quickly as she could, she skittered backwards over the rough cavern until she had backed up against one of the curved walls, scraping the palm of her hand in the process. "Stay there," she demanded, praying that her voice didn't sound as pathetic to the man as it did to her own ears. "You just stay right there, don't come any closer."

Tilson, peeking over the rock he was hiding behind, took one glance at the newcomer and stood up straighter. "Einar, is that you?"

The short man raised a calloused hand to mostly cover his eyes, trying to see beyond the bright light. In a gravelly voice, he responded. "Eh? What's that? Would you turn down your darned light? I can't see anything with you shining it at me like that."

Tilson scampered over forward, weaving between stones as he went. "I am Tilson," he pointed behind him, "and this is Morgan. The council sent us to investigate." Slipping on a patch of loose stone, he slid a couple feet before catching himself and continued. "We are here to look for clues to Cinderflare's disappearance."

Morgan turned the flashlight so that it was no longer directly focused on Einar. Since Tilson appeared to trust the man, or whatever he was, Morgan had no choice but to trust the haltija. She pointed the light down at the cavern floor and approached the pair of fey.

Once the light was no longer blinding him, Einar lowered his hand from his face, letting Morgan get a good look at him. His face was just as craggy as the rock he had just climbed out of, and even his eyes were a dusty grey color.

The expression on his weathered face showed that he wasn't too optimistic about their ability to find anything new but he seemed willing to let them try. He stepped further away from the rubble through which he had entered and smoothed the dust from his beard. "Well, we have gone over this cave pretty well and we did not find much, but if you're thinking you can do better, you're welcome to try."

Morgan and Tilson began poking around the

cavern, followed at a respectful distance by Einar. Morgan occasionally picked up a stone here and there but soon put them back down, deciding that they didn't mean much to the investigation. She looked over the walls of the cavern, still wondering if this was going to do any good at all. More than that, she was more certain than ever that this was no dream. It didn't feel like any dreams she had ever had before. Maybe there really was a council of fey out there that needed her help. She just hoped that she would be able to come through for them.

After a while, however, she was having serious doubts about her ability to help the fey with their disappearing dragons. "I still don't know what I'm supposed to be looking for. I can't even tell that this was a dragon's lair."

Einar harrumphed into his beard, folded his stubby arms, and leaned against a section of the wall. "You humans can't seem to see what's directly in front of you. From what I understand, your people think that this mountain is just a volcano, and not even a very dangerous one at that." He paused, and seemed to consider his words. "Well, you didn't think it was very dangerous 'til the dragon was attacked. Then your people fled, getting as far away as quick as they could."

Morgan's curiosity got the better of her and she had to ask. "So what are dragons like? Are they really as big as humans think they are?"

"Bigger. Most of 'em wouldn't even fit inside this cave but Cinderflare was a bit on the small side. Mean, too, so far as I've heard."

Morgan paused in her search to listen to him. "Mean?" She thought back to Tilson's assurance that dragons didn't attack people, not sure if she believed it. "Do dragons ever eat people?"

"Not usually. Mostly they hunt deer and elk, large land animals. I know that a lot of 'em prefer moose but I have heard that there were a few that liked humans too." The stocky man stopped to scratch his beard, dislodging a large clump of dirt. "Haven't heard of any of 'em going for humans lately, though. The council told 'em all a while ago that they weren't allowed to eat humans anymore, and I think most of 'em go along with what the council says." He looked back up at Morgan again and shrugged.

"So if any of 'em are still eating humans, they wouldn't exactly announce it, now would they?"

Morgan stared at Einar in surprise. Although Tilson had said that dragons weren't any danger to humans, what Einar had just said made it sound more like they could be really dangerous after all. She thought about all of the missing people that were talked about on the news, wondering how many of them were victims of a dragon attack.

That thought brought her back to the reason she was there in the first place and she remembered that Einar had also mentioned that all of the humans left when the dragon was attacked... If the humans left, maybe there was another reason for Cinderflare's disappearance. "Why did they leave when the dragon was attacked? I thought humans couldn't know about all this stuff."

"Well, they can't, not really. But they can come up with their own explanations for things that happen around 'em. I think they called this an 'eruption,' but they didn't really understand what was going on."

"An eruption? You mean I'm standing inside a volcano?" Morgan stepped back a couple paces toward the exit, looking at Einar in a combination of amazement and shock.

Einar shook his head. "Just like a human. Just 'cause I say 'eruption,' you start jumping to conclusions. Were you not listening? What the humans thought was an eruption was the battle between Cinderflare and whomever, or whatever, attacked 'im. It started smoking again a little while ago 'cause the young'ns hatched, and they were attacked too! That's why the council come and put me here, by the way."

"The council put you here? I thought you lived here."

"Ach, no. I don't live here, I'm just staying here, looking for clues, same as you. I am the guardian of Cinderflare's lair 'til he comes back, or 'til the council recalls me home." He shuddered. "There's no way I would want to live this close to a dragon. To one of them, I be meal sized."

Morgan nodded. It made an amount of sense, although she couldn't imagine what would be able to eat someone as tough-looking as Einar.

She went back to examining the walls and the floor. Although she was holding the light steady and looking closely, she could still not see any evidence of what had happened to the dragon.

Now that she thought about it, she couldn't even find any evidence that there had ever been a dragon living here. When she asked Einar about this, the fey chuckled and pointed to the long cracks that crisscrossed the cavern that she had noticed previously.

"You humans refer to these as 'vents,' I do believe. Truth be told, they be claw marks, from Cinderflare's claws, as 'e fought off the attack." After giving Morgan a chance to examine the scratches on the walls, he indicated to a pile of stones along the floor beneath the heaviest concentration of gouges. The stones were all broken open, revealing tiny shining crystals inside, lining the interior of the stones. "Ever see these before, lassie?"

Morgan took a good look at them and nodded. She recognized them; her dad had a few of them at home. "These are thunder eggs, they're everywhere around here."

Einar laughed, a deep, bellowing sound.

"Aye, they be eggs alright, just not from thunder. They be Cinderflare's eggs. They be all broken 'cause the young'ns hatched a few months ago."

Morgan bent to pick up one of the eggs. "These are real dragon eggs?" Her eyes widened in astonishment as she looked over the broken shell. It was almost too big to fit in the palm of her hand, larger by far than any of her dad's. The outside of the egg was coarse stone but there were clear shards of crystal inside. "Can I keep a piece?"

Einar shrugged and Tilson didn't seem to have any opinion, so Morgan tucked the fragment of eggshell into her jacket pocket. Turning back to the search, she tried to look at the cave through the eyes of a fey, tried to see things as her new friends would, but she still didn't see anything that would lead back to whatever had attacked the dragon.

She examined the gouges on the wall, remembering that they had come from the claws of the cave's owner, and decided that the dragon had to be huge. No human she knew of could have carried a dragon out of the cave, willing or not. Even if the human had assistants and a few huge helicopters, Morgan doubted that it would be possible.

Einar and Tilson were off a distance from Morgan and she could barely make out parts of their conversation. She wasn't paying much attention to what they were discussing until she overheard Einar raise his voice to Tilson. "No, I haven't been able to look in there; does it look like I'd be able to fit through that crack?"

Morgan immediately headed over to where the pair stood, listening to the two argue as she approached.

"Well, I'm not going in there, who knows what's inside." The haltija crossed his arms and shook his head. "No way. Besides, that's what the chosen is for, anyways." He uncrossed his arms and turned towards Morgan. "Hey, I think we found something!"

The fey were looking at a narrow crack in the wall, only about a foot wide. Looking at Einar, she could understand why the stocky man wouldn't be able to fit through it. "Why can't you just dig into it like you did back there?" She gestured towards the mound of stones where they had encountered him.

"Different kind of stone over here. It has too much quartz in it so's I can't get through it without dropping the whole cavern down." Einar shrugged. "It's kind of like a support column."

Morgan didn't quite understand but she was reasonably sure that she would be able to fit through the narrow opening. At the very least, she was willing to give it a try. She shone the light through first, just to be sure that it didn't just dead-end a few feet inside. The light played over loose stones and gravelly deposits, but Morgan could tell that there was more space inside that the light couldn't get to. She took off her jacket and dropped it on the floor just inside the main cavern, not wanting to get snagged and stuck on her way through the crack. Taking a deep breath and turning sideways, she began to squeeze through the sharp stones.

Just as she had been afraid of, she felt the fabric of her sweater snag on the stone behind her, and knew as soon as she heard the fabric tear that her mother was not going to like this, not one bit. At least the sweater had torn free and she wasn't stuck halfway through.

She could hear Einar and Tilson arguing outside. Einar was telling Tilson that he should be inside the crevice with Morgan, but Tilson was arguing right back. "I am her guide, not her guardian. Going into dangerous places like that isn't my job; that's why we have a chosen.

"Besides, I need to wait out here to report to the council if she finds something. If she gets stuck or hurt in there, I need to be able to get help, and I can't do that if I am in there too."

The argument faded at that. Morgan could hear Einar grumbling about cowardly haltijas, which seemed to offend Tilson because his voice turned squeaky and Morgan could no longer understand what he was saying. Carefully, she made her way through the jagged opening, which led to a smaller chamber.

The floor was littered with the same type of loose stones as those in the previous cavern but there were patches of dirt as well. Scattered across the floor were a few small piles of dirt, about six inches tall and just as wide. Realizing that finding mounds of loose soil inside an active volcano had to be unusual, Morgan knelt down next to one and began to poke through the mound.

With one hand, she held the flashlight with the beam trained on the pile that she was digging at. With the other, she scooped out handfuls of loose soil and let it sift through her fingers. She didn't find anything unusual in the first pile of dirt, but that didn't stop her. She moved over to the next pile, and then to the next pile after that.

While she was looking through the fourth pile, she discovered something, perhaps something important. When she reached back into the mound for the second scoop, her hand touched something that was solid, smooth, and very, very hot.

Stifling a gasp, she pulled her hand back and examined her fingers. Whatever it was hadn't been quite hot enough to blister her fingers but perhaps she just hadn't been in contact with it long enough to do that much damage. Standing up, she used the toe of her sneaker to move around the dirt, exposing the strange object.

It was a small ball, about two inches in diameter. Bright cardinal red, vibrant scarlet, deep burgundy, and dark maroon all churned through the orb, moving and dancing and shifting around in the confined space. Rather than reflecting the light of the flashlight as a normal glass ball should, this sphere seemed to absorb the light, drawing it into itself.

Morgan knelt down onto the ground next to the strange ball to have a closer look. Sure enough, the closer the flashlight got, the less light reflected off of it. She brushed some more of the dirt away from it, careful not to touch it bare-handed again. Morgan unrolled the sleeve of her sweater and pulled it down over her hand before she even tried to pick it up.

Through the fabric, she could still feel the heat but it was no longer as searing as it had first been against her bare fingertips. She shined the light on it again and peered into it but was still not able to tell what, if anything, was inside. After giving the cavern another cursory glance, she headed back to where the pair of fey waited.

Tilson scampered to her first, all but crawling up the leg of her jeans in excitement. "You found something! I knew you would find something. What is it? What did you find?" He perched on her shoulder and peeked down her arm.

"Just hang on a second, and I'll show you." Morgan walked towards Einar and opened her sweater-covered hand. "Do either of you have any idea what this is?"

Einar took the sphere bare-handed, Morgan noticed, but his hands were so calloused that he probably didn't notice the heat as much. He held it up close to his eyes and looked deep within its depths. "Never seen anything like this before." He looked down at Tilson. "I think you better notify the council. Looks like the lass found something important after all."

The haltija oohed and aahed over the swirling globe for a moment after Einar handed it back to Morgan before jumping back down to the ground and scampering towards the exit. He skittered and slipped along the piles of loose rock that were scattered around the cavern floor, his tail twitching furiously to maintain balance as he ran.

Morgan watched him disappear, and then

looked back to Einar. "Do you have anything that I can carry this in? It's kind of hot."

Einar nodded and disappeared into one of the dark tunnels that Morgan could only assume led further into the mountain. "Lair," she corrected herself. Since all of this seemed more real by the moment, she might as well call the cavern what it was. She grinned to herself, more excited than she could remember ever having been before.

She was standing inside a dragon's lair.

Alone, Morgan paced across the cavern, looking into the sphere and wondering what it was, what the significance of her find might be. She also wondered if the sphere was simply an accidental discovery. If that was the case, she hoped she might be able to keep it. Even if it was useless in the investigation, it looked neat.

She looked deep into the sphere and watched the colors swirl around. As she watched them, she could feel herself being drawn into the hypnotic patterns inside the sphere. Deeper and further into the colors she fell, forgetting where she was and what she was here for. Her mind was filled with flowing reds and she wasn't sure exactly why.

She heard a sound from deeper in the cavern where Einar had disappeared, a sound much like heavy rocks rolling across the floor. At the sound, she shook herself, blinked her eyes a number of times and looked away from the strange orb, not sure that she liked the sensation. She closed the sleeve of her sweater over the ball, just in case she was tempted to stare at it again.

Despite the noises she had heard deeper inside the mountain, Tilson returned first. "The council is very interested in what we found, so they will send for us when they can all get together again."

"Okay. Do you have any idea how long that might take?"

Tilson took a breath and spoke in the slow, clear voice again. "I am not a member of the council. I just report to them. You aren't a member either, and neither is Einar. Askel might be, but I doubt it, and he probably wouldn't tell us if we asked. Council members don't usually go around telling everyone that they are a member of the council, it's usually very hush-hush. So you should be happy that they decided to meet with you at all."

The miniature fey climbed up Morgan's clothes and perched on her shoulder, peering down at the sphere. "It is an honor, you know." When Morgan didn't reply, he continued. "Meeting with the council. Usually, a chosen won't meet the council of fey until after a couple months or so, when they have decided if the human is going to be able to work with us. So for them to be willing to meet with you already, it's a pretty big honor."

Morgan just nodded and went back to staring into the gloom. Einar returned and handed over a small leather pouch. Morgan thanked him and somewhat reluctantly tucked the sphere safely inside. "I guess that means it's time to go home then, hmm?"

Morgan and Tilson spent a few minutes saying their goodbyes to Einar before heading back out of the cave. For as long as they had spent underground, Morgan had half-expected to see the sun already up, but it was still fully dark. She carried the leather pouch and Tilson over to where Askel waited and climbed onto his back. She stroked Askel's feathers for a moment before saying, "All right, I think we're ready to go."

The flight home was smooth and steady. Morgan kept a tight hold onto the pouch, thinking about the strange adventure that the fey had just invited her into. She wondered again about the significance of the orb; even with her eyes closed she could still see the swirling colors and feel the heat radiating off of the sphere.

She settled down against Askel's strong neck and felt the wind blow past her, letting her thoughts wander and knowing that she couldn't tell her parents or anyone else about this; they would just tell her that it had all been a dream. She settled into the steady beat of the gryphon's wings, marveling at all that had happened in just this one short night.

Before she realized it, Tilson was shaking her awake because they had landed on the grass behind her house, just inside the little grove of trees.

~ 4 ~

COUNCIL

A few days went by and Morgan got back to the task of daily living. Tilson and the rest of the fey were nowhere to be seen and Morgan almost started to think that the entire night had been nothing more than a really strange dream. Whenever she started to wonder, however, all she had to do was peek into the leather pouch that Einar had given her.

Although the sphere was nowhere near as hot as it had been that first night, it was still quite warm to the touch and often Morgan just sat and held it, usually keeping it in its protective leather pouch and remembering how it felt the last time she had looked into its depths and watched the colors swirl.

She didn't get the sensation of falling into it again like she had before and she wondered if that was just her imagination, or maybe it didn't work the same way in the human world.

On the evening of the third day after her exploration of Cinderflare's lair, Morgan was in her bedroom, lying flat on her stomach on the wooden floor, her head propped on her hands as she stared at the rough leather pouch that contained the orb. She was supposed to be working on her history homework but the multicolored globe was a lot more interesting. She had been lying there for over an hour, deep in thought and wondering how far she would fall into the swirling colors if she took out the sphere to have another look, when she felt a small weight drop onto the center of her back. Turning her head slightly, she looked over her shoulder to see Tilson.

"We have to go," the haltija said, "without delay. The council is gathering. Do you have the sphere?" Tilson climbed further up Morgan's back to peer over the girl's shoulder. "Good. Let's be off, then."

"Where are we going?"

"Zea Island, where the council meets. Hurry, we need to go."

Morgan rolled onto her side, carefully spilling Tilson onto the rug beside them. She climbed to her feet and stretched before bending down to pick up the pouch. "Okay. I just have to make sure that Mom and Dad know I'm going to bed so they don't wonder where I am." She set the pouch onto the edge of her bed and headed for the stairs.

In the living room, she found her parents on the couch, watching a movie on TV. As was their habit, they were stretched out, feet on the coffee table and snacking on a big bowl of popcorn with cheddar sprinkles.

Morgan flopped into a chair where they would be sure to see her, and yawned deeply. Curling into a comfortable position in the chair, she laid her head on the armrest and began to relax, looking for all appearances as though she was starting to drift to sleep.

At the next commercial break, her mother

looked up to see Morgan drowsing. Gently, she spoke to her. "Sweetheart, why don't you go on up to bed? You look like you are about to fall asleep there."

Morgan made a few feeble protests before heading back to her room. She tucked her extra blanket under the covers to make it look like she was asleep in the bed. Quietly gathering up her now-ruined sweater, shoes and the flashlight that she had neglected to return to the drawer in the kitchen, she picked up the pouch and made her way quietly down the stairs, being careful to step as closely to the wall as she could to avoid the squeaky parts. Three steps from the bottom, the stair let out a groan that was practically deafening to Morgan and she froze, hoping that her parents hadn't noticed.

After a few racing heartbeats, she decided that they must not have noticed the sound and hurried down the rest of the steps.

Since her parents were in the living room, she snuck towards the kitchen, where she silently opened the back door just far enough to squeeze through before carefully closing it behind her with a barely audible click. Satisfied that her parents were unaware of her departure, she sat on the back steps and put on her shoes.

As she tied the laces, she looked up towards the line of trees and squinted slightly. The hazy form of Askel shimmered in the moonlight, more clearly visible than it had been the first time Morgan had seen him. Once her shoes were secured on her feet, Morgan picked up her flashlight and the pouch and skittered across the grass, snatching up Tilson in the process.

She had no idea what to expect at the council meeting they were headed to but she was looking forward to it nonetheless. Although she had only met a couple of fey since Tilson had approached her, she was curious to see what the others looked like. Not for the first time, she wondered of any of them looked anything like the ones in the fairy tales her mother used to read to her.

Askel lifted them into the air effortlessly and began to fly southeast, towards the Pentose River. As they got closer, Morgan noticed an island shimmering in the center of the river, where she had never noticed any island before.

She wondered if this was more of the fey magic or if she had just somehow never noticed the small mass of land. Remembering Tilson's explanation about how the fey used their magic to remain hidden from human sight, Morgan suspected it to be the former. Lower and lower they flew, until Morgan could almost reach out and touch the tops of the trees.

Askel headed directly towards a small clearing towards the center of the island, which was brightly lit from the moon overhead. As Askel circled to land, Morgan could see that they left a shadow along the ground beneath them. Somehow that surprised her, she had expected for their flight to leave no trace whatsoever. She wondered if they left a shadow as they flew any other time, but there wasn't any time to ask.

Askel landed with a soft thump on the grass and Morgan was surprised that she could see almost as well as if the sun had been up, instead of just the moon. She looked up and noticed tiny glowing lights twinkling among the branches of the trees surrounding the clearing, shining just brightly enough light to illuminate the area.

As Morgan dropped to the ground, she noticed a number of figures standing in the shadow of the trees that surrounded the clearing. Although she couldn't see most of them very well, Morgan could feel their attention focused on her. She stayed close to Askel's side; despite her previous excitement over being able to meet more of the fey, she was more than a little bit nervous about all of the attention and unsure of what was expected of her. She understood that she was here to meet with the council, but other than that, she was clueless.

Only a couple of moments had passed after the small group had landed in the clearing when Morgan noticed movement in one of the shadows surrounding them. She stepped closer to Askel and placed a hand on the feathers of his neck, watching as a figure stepped forward from the shadows and into the open to meet the arrivals.

He stood taller than Morgan, taller even than Morgan's father. His skin was a luminescent gold and his hair flowed long and silver. He wore a shirt that was the same twilight blue as the sky above them and pants the color of the river. Once he reached the middle of the clearing, where Morgan still stood with a hand on Askel's feathers, the stranger spread his hands wide and bowed. "Welcome. It is our pleasure for you to join us."

Not knowing how to react to this, Morgan turned to face him and tried to bow in return. "Thank you for inviting me." She couldn't bow quite as low as the fey had, since Tilson had dropped onto his customary place on Morgan's shoulder, and to bow as low as the tall fey had would have caused him to fall.

"I am Corran," the stranger said as he straightened again. "I speak for the council in matters involving humans. Please, follow me." He turned and walked back towards the edge of the clearing. He didn't look back to see if they were following, but continued speaking. "We have been informed that you found something of interest in Cinderflare's lair." At the edge of the trees, he turned back to the human and the haltija. "Could we see this item, please?"

Morgan reached into the pouch and pulled out the sphere. Holding it in her palm, she noticed that, although it had stayed warm while she had it at her house, it had been nowhere near as hot as it was when she had found it. Now, however, it was almost as hot as it had been in the mountain. She extended her hand towards Corran so that he could see it as well. Her hopes of being allowed to keep the orb faded quickly as she noticed the surprise in the fey's eyes.

Others moved in closer to get a look at the item in Morgan's hand as well and Morgan tried not to stare as they approached. The first to arrive was a small girl, barely two inches tall. She fluttered towards them on bright yellow and black wings that Morgan thought looked like those of the butterfly she had tried to draw not long ago. Three other girls soon joined her, one with blue wings, one with deep green wings and another with wings of light violet. All three perched on Morgan's outstretched arm, peering down at the orb. Morgan watched them land and wondered if these were fairies.

After the winged girls, another fey approached. At first, Morgan thought it was Einar, but when she looked closer, she was able to tell that this was not he. The stout man's beard was a slightly different color and there was no dirt and dust like Einar had been covered in. Also, this one was a bit taller, maybe by an inch or two, and had a long, jagged scar down the left side of his face, running from the front of his ear and disappearing into the beard on his chin.

Morgan almost thought the next fey to approach was a man riding on the back of a horse, until she noticed that the man and horse were the same creature. In movies, creatures that looked like that were called centaurs, but this one didn't quite look like those. Dark brown fur covered him from hooves to waist, where the fur turned to skin but did not change color. His face was clean-shaven except for a small patch of short, curly, and almost black hair sprouting from his chin. He nodded at Morgan as he approached, but did not speak.

Still others crowded in closer, leaning in or climbing onto others to get a better look. Some were gigantic, some tiny; some were vaguely human-looking and others obviously not so. Soon, Morgan was surrounded by fey so thickly that she could barely see beyond them to the clearing and Askel. She turned her attention back to Corran.

Corran made no move to take the sphere, but leaned in closer in order to see it more clearly. "Tell me, exactly how did you find this, and where?" As Morgan recounted her story, the fey nodded. "It seems that the danger we face is greater than we had believed."

"I thought you said it was pretty dangerous already."

Corran nodded and looked up to meet Morgan's eyes. "It was, but we had believed that the danger was mostly for the dragons, since they are the ones being targeted. Your discovery, while I am hesitant to voice my suspicions about its origins, tells me that there is a good chance that whoever is attacking the dragons may not be satisfied with just their removal."

Corran looked back at the sphere for a few long moments before continuing. "More of us may be targeted afterwards."

"What do you mean?"

Corran sighed. "Although I personally have never seen one of these before, nor were any known to exist in my father's lifetime, this orb of yours radiates with strong magic. Not just any magic, I must say, this feels like ancient magic. For thousands of years, the knowledge of how to use the magic of the ancients has been hidden, buried so that none may use it, to keep this land safe from those with ill intent."

"So, someone found a way to use this old magic and they're using it against the dragons?" When Corran nodded, Morgan continued. "What makes you think that they'll come after others later?"

"I cannot say for certain." Corran looked away from the girl, barely hiding the expression of disgust. "But what I do know is that this magic was hidden for good reason in order to keep the entire world, both the human world and the world of fey, safe."

"Does this tell you anything about what's happening to the dragons?"

"It might," Corran admitted, "but I am not the one to decide that. Not being a dragon, of course I am not as well versed in the means and ways of them. There is, however, one dragon remaining in the council, he should have a better idea of what this means."

Morgan followed Corran into the trees. Just beyond the clearing was a wide but overgrown trail. They followed this trail as it wound towards the edge of the island, where it ended at a tunnel. "Follow this path, it will lead you to Stormshock's grotto. Be careful to stay on the path, however, for he does not like for others to tread on his grasses."

The bushes and ivy from the trees grew thick here and joined together overhead, barely letting any light from the sky beyond. Morgan looked at the tall fey. "Isn't Tilson coming with me?"

"Not this time. We have a great number of questions for him so it is best that he remains here to answer them." He looked towards the tunnel that he had indicated for her to follow. "Also, Stormshock is very private and prefers as few visitors as possible at one time."

Morgan nodded, took a deep breath, and tucked the ball back into the leather pouch, holding the small bundle tight. If she tripped over a root or other obstacle, she didn't want to drop and lose it in the darkness. Remembering Corran's warning, she didn't want to discover what would happen should she have to go searching for the missing sphere if it rolled off the path. Straightening her back and exhaling slowly, she stepped into the gloom.

The trees grew closer together, crowding against the narrow trail so tightly that Morgan could easily have reached out a hand and touched them on either side simultaneously. They were still covered in moss, ivy, and all sorts of climbing vines, which hung down from the branches overhead to brush against Morgan's hair. She pulled the pouch tighter, clutching it against her chest as she nervously walked deeper into the gloom. No movement rustled the foliage around her, no birds called to each other overhead. Morgan had never felt as profound a sense of loneliness as this before and she knew that the sensation would not easily be forgotten.

She wished that Corran had come with her, or maybe Askel. Even Tilson, with all of his silly chatter, would have been a welcome companion.

As she walked further, Morgan began to shiver. Although the temperature had not dropped since she had entered the tunnel, she still felt cold. The path that she walked on had not become any narrower but the trees on either side seemed to press in towards her, closer and ever closer, until Morgan had to reach out a hand to touch a tree, partly to convince herself that all of this was real and partly to reassure herself that the trees were not going to suffocate her. The small hairs along the back of her neck began to tingle and Morgan felt as though thousands of eyes were watching her, motionless and hidden in the shadows.

Barely any light was able to fight its way through the dense covering of the path but Morgan was able to see just well enough in the meager glow to follow the trail in the gloom without having to pull out her flashlight. Instead, she tucked the orb into the waistband of her jeans and held the flashlight tightly in both hands, just in case she needed to be ready to defend herself against whatever was watching her.

After walking for far longer than she thought she could have, beyond where she should have hit the edge of the island, the trees began to widen apart again and the vines that covered them began to recede. Instead of the light of the moon, as had lit the clearing where she had left Tilson and Askel, bright sunshine blinded Morgan. She had to loosen her grip on the flashlight to shade her eyes, surprised by the sudden change in light. Overhead, the trees opened once more to reveal a clear, bright purple sky. Beneath, the ground was softer here, as moss covered the path and...

"Wait, purple?" Morgan asked herself, and looked back up to the sky. Sure enough, the sky was a light but rich purple, almost the shade that her mother referred to as violet. As she walked, staring up at the alien sky, Morgan couldn't help but wonder exactly where she was. Before she could continue much further along in her thoughts however, the trees opened even more, the path leading out into a clearing that was much larger than the one from which she had first entered the tunnel.

The clearing was carpeted with flowers, tiny blooms in white, blue and yellow in a field of deep green. The path took a sharp turn to the right immediately as it left the tree-lined tunnel and began to circle the clearing. The moss covering the path was much thicker, causing every step Morgan took to feel as though she was walking on a mattress filled with sand. Morgan followed it, trying to look both ahead along the moss-covered path and into the center of the clearing at the same time. In the very center of the clearing towered a group of large rocks, but there was no sign of any dragons.

On the one hand, she was almost hoping that the dragon wasn't home but on the other hand, she would be disappointed at having come all the way out here only to discover that it was gone. Not until the night of Tilson's arrival had she ever even considered the possibility of meeting a real dragon and the possibility of missing out on that event was disappointing, to say the least. The only way to find out for certain whether or not the encounter was to happen, she realized, was to keep walking.

The path wound around and around, spiraling in closer to the center with each pass. Much as Morgan wanted to leave the spiral path, she absolutely did not want to bring the ire of the dragon so she restrained herself from hasty action. Finally, she reached the end of the path, where there was still no dragon to be found.

The path ended at the pile of rocks she had noted from the entrance, so all Morgan could think to do was to look closer. She climbed onto the boulders in front of her, climbing higher and higher off the ground. When she finally reached the top, she discovered that the rocks were not just a large pile as they had appeared from the entrance of the clearing but were instead a ring around a pool of deep, clear water. Lounging in the pool was the largest creature that Morgan had ever seen, which she immediately knew must be the dragon.

~ 5 ~

STORMSHOCK

The dragon had an elegant body with a long, slender tail and neck. It was covered with fine metallic scales the rich green color of jade. Its short, thin limbs had three closely-mounted toes on each foot, each ending in sharp talons, much like those of a bird. Large leathery wings, also jade green but with darker green scales along the bony ridges, ran from its shoulders to its hips. A row of tall spines chased from the base of its skull down its back to the tip of its tail. The dragon's head was narrow, with small oval nostrils perched high and far back on its snout, which was surrounded by bony knobs.

Morgan stopped, afraid to approach any closer. Even mostly submerged in the water, the dragon still managed to loom above her; its head alone was bigger than Morgan. Before she had a chance to turn about and leave the great dragon to its rest, however, one giant eye cracked open and focused on the girl.

"Ah, you are here. I was wondering how long it would take before the council deemed it safe for us to meet." The dragon turned its head to look at Morgan more squarely. "Not quite what I had expected to see in the chosen one, but I suppose you will do." Its voice was low and it spoke slowly, carefully pronouncing every word.

Morgan tried to stammer out something in response, anything at all, but after a few failed attempts she decided that to simply nod would be a safer means of communication.

"Not too talkative, are we? Well, I think that's a good quality to have. Most humans, they seem to prattle on about this and that, not even really seeming to care about what they are saying so long as someone is listening." The dragon reached up with one of its feet and tapped a couple of claws against a boulder closer to the pool. "Come, have a seat, girl."

When Morgan hesitated, the dragon moved back a bit, raised a few stories into the air, and appeared confused. "I am not going to eat you, if that is your concern. I merely wish to get to know you a bit better and perhaps discover what it is about you that the council deems so important. Come now, have a seat, and we can talk."

Cautiously, Morgan approached and climbed down into the rocky border of the pool. She stepped onto the boulder that the dragon had indicated and hesitantly took a seat. The dragon settled back down a bit at this, sinking slightly deeper into the water and arranging itself to be comfortable. "Now then, let's just start at the beginning, shall we? I assume you have a name; I believe humans are doing that now?"

"Morgan. My...my name is Morgan." Her voice was hoarse, as her mouth had gone dry a while ago. She tried to swallow a few times, without much improvement.

The dragon nodded. "That's good, we are getting somewhere now. Polite conversation generally starts with introductions. My name is Stormshock." When Morgan made no indication of recognizing the name, Stormshock shook his head and made a noise that could only be described as a snort. "Humans," he muttered to himself. "They never were very good at remembering things."

When Morgan only blinked in confusion, Stormshock continued. "It does not matter. But tell me, what progress have you made in discovering what has befallen my kin?"

"I...I'm not really sure. I found something in Cinderflare's mountain, something Corran said that you should see. That's why I was sent to you; the council said that you'd have a better idea of what it is and what it means."

As Morgan reached for the pouch at her belt, Stormshock leaned in closer, obviously interested to see what she had found. When Morgan pulled out the orb and held it up so that it could be more easily seen, however, Stormshock recoiled. His eyes widened in surprise and his mouth opened and the scales pulled back, showing off his sharp fangs. "Where did you find that?" he asked in a hiss.

Morgan merely whimpered. She had nowhere to run, nowhere to hide, had no idea where she was, and now it looked like the dragon was about to eat her for doing what she had been sent to do. Her stomach clenched tightly and she could feel every muscle in her body tensing, ready to flee. She was shaking almost uncontrollably, barely managing to keep hold of the sphere. Without realizing it, she had scooted herself backwards a distance so that she was about to fall off the rock she had just climbed onto. She looked around, trying to find a place that she could run to before she was eaten, but there was nowhere to go.

"Calm down, girl. I said I am not going to eat you, and I meant it." Stormshock's voice came out in more of a growl or maybe a snarl than before but the sound was somehow less threatening than the shocked hiss had been.

Morgan dared a glance back at the huge dragon, and swallowed again. "I...It..." she stammered, "It was in the...Cinderflare...in the cave." She swallowed again. "There was a room, the opening was too small for Einar to get through...I was able to get in."

"Calm down, girl. I am not going to hurt you; I am beginning to wonder how many times I will have to tell you that. Just sit back here where I can see you better, take a good couple breaths, and start at the beginning."

There was nothing that Morgan wanted less at that particular moment than to move closer to the angry dragon but she couldn't see any way around it without being insulting. Hesitantly, she scooted forward until her feet were hanging over the front of the rock. She took a few deep breaths, swallowed a few times to clear her throat, and told the dragon everything. She explained about her first meeting with Tilson, about being led out to meet with Askel, flying to the volcano, and about the conversations she had had with Einar while looking for clues. She described the grooves on the walls of Cinderflare's lair and the egg shells that Einar had shown her. She described the crack in the wall that she had squeezed through, catching her sweater on the rocks, poking around in the dirt to find the sphere, and how hot it had been.

Stormshock remained quiet through the

telling, merely nodding his head at certain points. Whenever he nodded, however, Morgan went into greater detail about what she saw, heard, smelled, everything. She wasn't sure whether or not any of the details mattered but she was absolutely positive that she didn't want to anger the dragon again by overlooking a critical point just because she hadn't realized its importance.

"It was just lying there, buried under the dirt... I didn't know what it was, Einar said he didn't know either, but he gave me the pouch to put it into because it was so hot. So I took it home, and kept it safe like Einar and Tilson said to until I was called to the meeting here. Well, I wasn't expecting the meeting here, but the meeting with the council, I mean. When I showed it to Corran, he got really surprised and then sent me here to you. That's all I know, I swear."

Stormshock held out a massive paw. "Give me the globe. I will keep it safe until we are able to decide what to do with it."

Morgan gave him the orb and watched as Stormshock moved to the other side of the pool and put it away. "What is it? Corran didn't seem to know, and neither did Einar."

After making sure that the sphere was safe, Stormshock turned back to Morgan, looking surprisingly sad. "It is magic, trapped. That orb holds the essence of Cinderflare, all that she once was."

Morgan blinked. "I don't understand."

"Of course you do not." replied Stormshock. "But I can explain, at least in part." He moved back into about the same position he had been when Morgan had arrived, and got comfortable before continuing.

"First, you must understand that we fey are all magical. That is to say, we are made of magic. We are born of magic and we exist because of the magic within us. When we die, all that we once were passes back into the magical field that covers our world, which we call the ether. From there, we are born anew into a new creature, into a new life."

Morgan nodded, somewhat understanding.

"This magic all around us," explained the dragon "is what causes us to exist, what allows us the abilities we have, and it keeps the veil between your world and ours in place. Without this magic, I would not exist, nor would Corran, Einar, Tilson, or any of the others that you have met or will meet. Without the magic, all that would be left here is your people, the humans."

"So that sphere I found is really just a ball of magic?"

"Well, yes and no. I cannot deny that it is a ball of magic, but it is a ball of magic that has been trapped. In essence, it has been removed from the ether and cannot move on to where it needs to go.

"Think of it as like a soul. You humans still believe in souls, do you not?" When Morgan nodded, he continued. "You see, Cinderflare's soul is trapped inside that orb. She cannot move on to her next life until we find a way to release her, to free her. Do you see?"

Morgan nodded again, appalled at what she had just been told. Of all the things she had guessed the sphere to be, a trapped soul wasn't one of them. She couldn't think of much that was more horrifying. "So how do we get him back out of there?"

Stormshock chuckled. "Well, first of all, Cinderflare is a *she*, not a he. Secondly, I am not sure how to release her, but I will see what I can find out. There must be a way."

"What can I do to help?"

"Find the rest of the spheres. If this is the fate that befell Cinderflare, it stands to reason that the same happened to the others. Find their orbs and bring them to me. I will safeguard them. When I find a way to release them from this prison that they are in, I will let you know."

Morgan nodded again. "Does all of this tell you anything about who, or what, might've done this?"

"Not yet. I am sure that we will find out in time, but for now, it remains a mystery."

"What about the rest of the fey? Corran said that this meant that the rest of the fey were in danger as well."

"Of that, I have no doubt," Stormshock responded. "Anything powerful to do this to a dragon is more than powerful enough to do the same to the elvor like Corran."

"Elvor...is that what he is?"

Stormshock simply nodded. "I believe your people call them elves."

Somehow, she had always thought that elves would be shorter. "What about Einar, what is he?"

"He is a dvergar. You would likely know him as a dwarf."

Morgan nodded; she had heard of those as well. "That reminds me. There are a lot of things about you that we humans know about. How can we know so much, if we've always been separated like we are now?"

"That's because we weren't always separate, you see. A long time ago, before my time so it was a long time ago indeed, the humans lived side by side with the fey. We were aware of you, and you were aware of us."

"So what happened?"

Stormshock sighed before answering. "The humans grew to be greedy. They were arrogant and started to take over everything. War parties of humans attacked the peaceful fey around them, to take the lands that they were living on, to take all of what the fey had. Some of the humans learned how to manipulate the ether to possess magic of their own. During all this, the fey almost died out completely.

"That was when the First Council was created. Representatives of all the different races of fey gathered together in secret from the humans, to try and find a solution. After a long time, with much bickering and arguing among them, it was finally decided that the only way to continue our existence was to become separated completely from the humans. We would remove ourselves from their lives and start to lead our own again. So the veil was created."

"So, if the fey and the humans are completely separate, how am I here? How was I able to go from my world to yours?"

"That is because we are no longer completely separate. You see, since we are made of ether, all of the ether was locked away on our side of the veil. Unfortunately, this meant that the humans no longer had any magic left in their world and a lot of unexpected problems came of this as well.

"Until the separation, we hadn't been aware that humans were dependent on the ether also, just not to the same extent as we are.

"After a number of years and much debate in the council, it was decided that we would need to have some sort of communication and transfer of energy between the worlds. By then, however, very few humans still believed in us, for we had become nothing more than myths to them. We found that the easiest ones to work with were those still young enough to believe in things that the older ones no longer did."

"So there have been others like me?"

Stormshock laughed. "Of course there have been others. There have been ongoing relationships between the fey and the humans for a very long time. But, over time, many of the humans that we have worked with have decided to distance themselves from us in order to lead a normal life in your world. Each time that happens, it becomes time to send out the scouts to find someone new that will be open to us."

"So that's how you found me, then?"

Stormshock nodded. "It is highly likely that you were being monitored long before Tilson approached you, just to be sure that no mistakes would be made, as had been made with a few chosen in the past."

Morgan thought back to the butterfly that had seemed to lead her home and all of the noises that had haunted her after moving into her new house. She wondered if the butterfly was actually one of the fairies she had just seen out in the clearing. Suddenly, everything made a lot more sense. "What kind of mistakes?"

Stormshock's eyes widened a bit and he sat back quickly, sending a wave of water from his pool over the rocks behind him. "Don't worry about that; it doesn't concern you. For now, all you have to worry about is finding more orbs and bringing them to me."

"But..."

"You should be heading back to the council soon. I am sure that someone out there will be wondering where you are if you are not back where you belong soon."

Understanding that Stormshock would not say anything further, Morgan climbed back down from the rocks around the pool. She took a moment to stretch before heading along the winding path back to the council.

~ 6 ~

SNOWBOUND

Morgan was beyond tired. Over the last week, she had been to six different lairs, argued with ten different guardians, and had found a good dozen spheres to bring back to Stormshock. Since Einar had accused Tilson of being a coward for not wanting to help Morgan look through the crack in the wall in Cinderflare's lair, she suspected that the council had spoken with Tilson while she was in her meeting with Stormshock about helping her more. He had followed her more closely while she was out on her searches, even if he was grumbling a lot more about doing so.

She had flown with Tilson and Askel across the country and back too many times to count and had barely been keeping up with her homework from school. Just staying awake in class was hard enough. Because most of the work she did with the fey happened at night, it was no surprise that she had gone to bed early one evening when Tilson came in.

"Pssst...Hey, sleepyhead Morgan! Wake up, it's time to go!"

Morgan just groaned and rolled over, pulling the blankets up over her head to block the noise.

Tilson grabbed an edge of the blanket and started to tug. "Come on, we gotta go. Askel's outside waiting for us."

Morgan rolled over to face the haltija. "Can't we have just one night off? I'm tired."

Tilson lost his grip on the blanket and fell backwards, falling off the edge of the bed with a thump. When Morgan looked over the edge to see if he was all right, she found the haltija flat on his back on the floor, glaring up at her.

"What? I didn't do that."

Tilson climbed to his feet. "Yes, you did. If I

hadn't had to tug on you so much, if you had just been ready to go like you were supposed to, that wouldn't have happened." His tiny voice even more shrill than usual, the haltija brushed invisible dirt off his clothes. "Lazy humans, never willing to get things done, even when they really need to get done."

Morgan sighed. There was no point in arguing with Tilson when he was in this kind of a mood; it never ended well. "Fine, fine, just give me a minute, will you? I still need to get dressed." She sat up and deliberately dropped the blanket on top of Tilson, who started sputtering again.

Ten minutes later, the pair was outside, crossing the field behind Morgan's house. She didn't even need to squint and look very hard to see Askel, standing in his customary place next to the trees. Since meeting Tilson and Askel for the first time, Morgan had been getting better about seeing through the veil between worlds. Most things were still pretty hazy and she knew that she was still not seeing a lot that was out there but she believed that she was getting better at it. Things that she had gotten used to, she had almost no difficulty in seeing. She was starting to realize that the more time she spent in the world of the fey, the easier seeing their world became.

Soon they were airborne, heading north again. Secure on Askel's back, lulled by the steady rise and fall of his wings, Morgan was soon fast asleep once more.

She awoke to Tilson, poking and tugging on the fingers of one of Morgan's hands. "What are you doing?" she mumbled.

"This is for you, the council sent it. They said it should help. Won't take away all of it, but you shouldn't die." As he spoke, Tilson got a firm hold on her hand and began to separate her fingers, pulling one out almost to the point of pain.

"What?" Fully awake now, Morgan sat up and was immediately blasted by a wave of frigid air. She immediately ducked back down, closer to Askel's body where the heat was radiating up. "Save me from what?"

Tilson took the opportunity to shove a small golden ring onto one of Morgan's fingers, pushing it up barely past the first knuckle before giving up. "The cold, O Intelligent One. Humans don't survive very well in the cold, so Corran sent that for you."

"Why didn't you tell me that we were heading to the cold? I would've grabbed my winter coat." She pushed the ring up onto her finger, surprised as it expanded to fit. Looking more closely at the ring, Morgan noticed that it was a very thin golden band with tiny clear stones set into the outer edge of it, small crystals that pointed away from her hand.

"Why didn't you tell me, she asks. Why hasn't she asked, any time we have gone out, where we are going? Why do I always have to be the only one that's actually prepared around here?" Tilson sank back down into Askel's warmth, crossed his arms, and shook his head.

"I'll tell you why, that's what I'll do. Somebody couldn't be bothered to get out of bed and be ready to go when we got here, that's why. So somebody is just going to have to deal without her winter coat, and be thankful that at least Corran was thinking ahead. Somebody had better just hope that ring does what it's supposed to do."

Morgan sighed and settled down against

Askel's warm back, tuning out the haltija, as she frequently did. Tilson continued to rant without saying anything really important and Morgan wasn't terribly interested in listening to him whine. Instead, she looked off to the side, to try and figure out where they were.

The ground below them stretched as far as she could see in every direction, great masses of white with few patches of life to be seen. Huge mountains of ice rose up to meet the pale clouds, one shade of white blending perfectly into the next against the backdrop of a deep black night sky. No birds flew up to play with Askel in the air, as had happened before. It was too cold here, wherever they were, to play.

They were heading for one of the icy peaks and it appeared to Morgan that Askel was planning to land them on the very top but that was not the case. Askel swooped down and landed at the base of the mountain, which was much more of a hill once they got closer, or maybe an iceberg. Again Morgan wondered, where were they?

After a moment of looking around, Morgan dropped to the ground and immediately fell to her back, her feet rocketing out from under her as if she had stepped on... well... ice.

Carefully, she stood back up, keeping a hand on Askel for support and trying to keep her feet under her this time. She looked to see how Askel was managing to not slide away and noticed that he had dug his claws into the ice, using them as anchors to keep him in place. For the first time in her life, Morgan wished that she had claws, too.

Once she was sure of her footing, she reached up to take Tilson and placed him in the hood of the sweater that she had gotten into the habit of wearing. It was more comfortable for Tilson, and it kept him out of Morgan's way while she was trying to work. She adjusted the neck to keep his weight from choking her and looked around.

Once they were ready, Morgan looked towards the hill, doubtfully. "H-h-how are w-w-we supposed to g-g-get to the lair f-f-from here?" she chattered. It took a great deal of effort to keep her teeth from clicking together as she spoke, she was shivering so much. She rubbed her hands together and blew into them, trying to warm them, to no avail. All she could do was stuff them onto the pockets of her sweater and pray she didn't need to catch herself again.

A deep, grating noise sounded from the hill and a section of the ground seemed to push out and move to the side. An enormous head with steel grey hair, bright blue eyes, and a beard that ran from his nose to his belt peeked out from behind the moving rocks. The entire slab was set down adjacent to the opening and the largest man that Morgan had ever seen stepped out from behind it.

He was dressed in dark blue robes that reached from his neck to his fingertips and down to where the fur-edged hem swept along the snow as he moved. "Come inside, come inside, it's blasted cold out here." Stepping aside, the huge man indicated that the group should enter before him.

Morgan followed Askel into the gloomy cave, looking up at the man as they passed. More than twice Morgan's height, the man certainly looked strong enough to move a small mountain.

Inside, the cave was not quite as gloomy as it had appeared from the outside. A small fire had been set in the center of the main cavern, bathing the room in a soft yellow-orange glow. Once the opening was closed behind them, Morgan could feel the warmth seeping into her, albeit slowly. She stepped closer to the fire to absorb more of its warmth, thankful to feel her fingers again.

"I was starting to wonder if you were going to make it or not, with that blizzard that hit a couple of hours ago. You must have just missed it." The giant stepped closer to the fire as well, and smiled down at Morgan. "You must be Morgan. I am Kun, guardian of Frostbite's lair." He offered a massive hand, which Morgan shook, her hand completely engulfed in the larger man's.

Kun explained that he had been guarding the cave since shortly after Frostbite's disappearance. He hadn't been in the cave, or even anywhere near it, before the dragon had been suspected missing. The council had contacted him to check on Frostbite but there had been nothing in the cave to find but ice. "I know that the dragons who live in places such as this like the cold, and I do too, but I think a body needs to have a bit of warmth now and again also." He looked back at the fire once more. "Besides that, maybe whatever it was that took Frostbite may not like fire, and having one here might be enough to keep them out."

Morgan wasn't sure what to say. She didn't believe that whoever was responsible for the missing dragons would stay away just because of a small fire like this one, but she also understood that the fey needed something to keep their hopes alive. Many guardians over the last week had expressed similar ideas and Morgan had tried to explain to the first couple that their actions probably wouldn't help, but it was pointless. Everyone needed to feel that they were doing something. Since whatever was attacking the dragons never seemed to return to the lairs she had already been to, Morgan had started to wonder if maybe the actions of the fey were helping after all. At the very least, it seemed to make them feel better.

When she had feeling back in her hands once more, Morgan turned back to Kun. "I guess you've already looked through the cave and didn't find anything?" When Kun nodded, she continued. "Are there any small places that you can't get into, any softer areas in the stone, er…ice?"

Kun thought for a few minutes and shrugged. "Not that I have noticed, but if there are any openings like that, they would be closer to the floor. I know there aren't any towards the ceiling. As for softer areas, I don't think there are any inside. There may be a patch or two outside but after that blizzard we just had, they would be buried under snow if they are there at all."

Morgan nodded. She looked over her shoulder at Tilson, who was no longer hunkered down in the hood of the sweater. Instead, he had moved as close to the fire as he could and was in the process of warming his tail. "I think we should check inside before heading back out into the cold. What do you think?" When the haltija nodded, Morgan looked around the icy cave. "You look over there, and I'll start looking over here. Let me know if you see anything, OK?"

The pair searched for hours, peeking under every loose piece of ice, poking at pockets of snow, and knocking and tapping at the walls to look for hollow areas that might have frozen closed once more. Tilson spent most of his energy running back and forth between the area that he was searching and the fire, taking many breaks to warm up. Askel and Kun stayed close to the fire as well, staying on the opposite side of the flames as the searching pair so that they didn't block the light.

They found nothing.

Tilson whimpered as Morgan spoke to Askel and Kun. "We have to look outside; that's the only place the sphere could be. It's not here, not anywhere in here."

Kun was not happy about letting the trio back out into the frozen exterior, but he kept the door open so that they could make frequent stops back inside to thaw. "Be careful out there," he cautioned her as she walked past. "A body can get frozen solid in just a few minutes if you're not cautious." He stayed near the entrance, waiting to see if any help would be needed from him.

Morgan and Tilson agreed to split up, reasoning that they would be able to cover a lot more ground separately. It also meant that the search would be over faster so that they could all get out of the snow and into a warmer area. Kun agreed to stay back and watch in order to be sure that neither of them wandered too far away from the opening of the lair. "Many people have gotten lost out there and never found again. It's easy to get disoriented with nothing but white around you, even easier to freeze to death trying to find your way back."

Morgan headed off to her left, scanning the ground as she went. She spotted some likely mounds of ice debris and started to poke around when she heard Kun speaking. It sounded as though the giant was berating Tilson for trying to sneak back into the cave so quickly. Morgan just chuckled to herself and continued the search.

The first mound she searched yielded no results, nor did the second or third. Just as she decided she was about ready to head back to the cave and start looking in a different direction, she stopped short when she heard the whispering voice.

"Are you lost?" The voice asked her. It was a woman's voice, soft and smooth. "You have come a far distance, young girl." Rather than coming in through her ears as normal sounds did, it seemed as though the voice spoke directly into her brain.

The entire world seemed to fade away, sounds of Kun and Tilson arguing faded, as Morgan turned to see a beautiful girl, not much older than she, walking towards her. She was dressed in a strange shimmering gown, mostly white but with gold patterns sewn into designs that Morgan couldn't quite identify. Her skin was the same color as the snow all around them and her hair was the darkest black that Morgan had ever seen. As the woman moved towards Morgan, she didn't seem to walk as much as she appeared to glide over the snow, leaving no marks where she had been.

Moments passed in a blur. Morgan could hear the woman speaking to her but she couldn't quite comprehend what was being said; all she could do was nod and move closer to her. Her voice was hypnotic, drawing her away from her friends, her mission, her everything. Dumbly, she moved further into the barren land, trying to reach her. She didn't know why she wanted to reach her. She just knew that she did. She had to.

The woman lifted a pale hand to beckon her closer and Morgan responded before she even realized what she was doing. Closer to her, she could hear her more clearly, still speaking directly into her mind, with the barest of movements from her lips. "Leave this desolate world of pain. Come with me and I will see you to safety."

She held out her arms to her and Morgan moved in to embrace her in return, not sure why it was so important that she did, just knowing that if she didn't reach her soon, she would…

A deafening roar echoed off the hills around her, and Morgan was shocked back into consciousness, even as she was hoisted high into the air. Huge hands held her around the waist and chest, pulling her away from the mysterious woman.

"No, Yuki! The child is not for you." Kun's voice barely registered in Morgan's ears, as they were still ringing from Kun's bellow. "Leave her be."

The woman's face contorted into a mask of rage as she shrieked at the giant in fury and a blast of snow appeared out of nowhere. The flakes swirled around, growing thicker by the second. Before Morgan could tell what was happening, the shrieking woman faded into the swirling mass and was gone from view. The twisting blizzard disappeared as well, moving over the land until it was far off in the distance, unable to be seen even from Morgan's high viewpoint.

Morgan shook her head, trying to clear out some of the fuzziness that still filled her brain. "What happened?" she asked Kun. "Who was that?"

"That was Yuki-onna. She is dangerous, one of the worst out here. She can lure people to be lost in the snow, only to be found dead later, or she can kill with a touch, freezing you where you stand. Many have died because of her." Kun carefully lowered the girl to the ground, keeping a steadying hand ready to catch her should she fall. "Are you all right?"

Morgan just nodded, still trying to clear out the cobwebs that had appeared in her head. She looked around and realized just how far away from Frostbite's lair the woman had lured her. "I just don't understand how I got this far away from you guys; I wasn't that far out." She blinked once, twice.

There, in the ice beneath the blizzard that had taken the mysterious woman, a white globe swirled.

Morgan dropped to her knees on the ground and started to dig. The orb was as cold as Cinderflare's had been hot, so some of the ice had frozen to it but Morgan was determined. After poking and prodding at the ice for a few minutes, she had an idea. She pulled the golden ring from her finger and pushed it down over the sphere, scraping the points of the miniature gems across the ice to push the ring further. She grunted and shoved, sweating even as she shivered from the biting chill that hit her as soon as the ring was removed.

Kun moved closer to her, sheltering her

from the wind as best he could with the heat of his body. Askel moved in close on the other side, forming even more of a barrier against the deadly cold.

Morgan could feel her cheeks burning hot as the freezing air drew the heat from her. Her fingers ached as they pushed and her breath clouded the air before her, making it difficult to see. Her nose burned and her eyes watered, but she kept pushing. Breathing was quickly becoming difficult, because the more cold air she sucked in, the harder it was to draw the next breath. Her face and hands felt like they were on fire and everything was swiftly going numb.

She struggled with her hands, trying to make her fingers do what they were supposed to, but they didn't want to cooperate. She lost her grip on both the ring and the sphere once, twice, and she knew that if she didn't get it soon, she wasn't going to be able to get it at all.

She needed this orb. Morgan wasn't sure why she needed this particular sphere so badly, but she knew that if she didn't get it now, it would be lost forever. Maybe the council would decide that she wasn't as good of a chosen as they had thought she was, and would find someone new to continue in her place. More than anything, Morgan didn't want that to happen, and she didn't even know why or when it had become this important to her.

Finally, she could feel the ring slide over the widest part of the sphere and taper back in again. Immediately, Morgan buried both hands deep in the ice, pulling against the frozen globe, tugging it free. When it finally came loose with an audible crack of breaking ice, she fell backwards into the snow, almost landing on Kun as she tumbled.

She shoved the ring back over her finger and held the sphere tight to her chest, shaking uncontrollably and praying that she wouldn't drop it.

Finally, she could feel the biting cold start to recede and she could breathe freely again as comforting warmth flooded into her body. She relaxed against Kun, exhausted.

~ 7 ~

ANCIENT

Morgan woke with a start, not knowing where she was. She was covered in a warm blanket and could feel something soft beneath her head. As she rolled over to her left side to get a better look at her surroundings, the familiar squeak of her mattress greeted her. She was home, safe in her bed. She cracked an eye to have a quick look around, checking to see if Tilson was there. Thankfully, she was alone.

She snuggled back down under her blankets and dozed for a little while, enjoying the feel of a good night's sleep. Her body still ached a bit from the night out in the cold but not as badly as it had been. She stretched her legs out, feeling the cool sheets rub against her legs, and settled back down for a few more hours' rest.

She had no idea how she had gotten back home or ended up in her bed again, but she didn't care. As long as she was here, she was going to enjoy it.

"This isn't happening," she muttered to herself as she felt something small, lumpy, and full of elbows drop onto her. She squeezed her eyes shut hoping that maybe, just maybe, it would work this time, but when she cracked an eye, there was Tilson. The haltija climbed off of Morgan and walked up to the pillow where he pressed down an indentation in the soft material and sat, staring intently at her from only a few inches away.

"No," Morgan groaned. "Today is my day off. No school, no spheres, just sleep." She rolled away from Tilson, fully aware that she would be pestered until she got out of bed. She always was. She had never met anyone that was as persistently obnoxious as Tilson. She pulled the blankets tighter around her head until only her nose peeked from between them and then reached her arms up to clasp the pillows around the blankets, over her ears. There was a thump, muffled by the layers of blanket and pillow around her head, but unmistakable. She might not have had a choice in getting up, but she wasn't about to make it easy.

"Come on, lazybones, get up." Tilson climbed onto the mound of blankets and began to poke at Morgan. "The council wants to see you. They sent me here to get you. Now come on and get up already!" After prodding at the blankets for a moment, Tilson found the spot he was looking for. Reaching one skinny arm back, he pointed two fingers and jabbed them into Morgan's side.

"Ouch!" Morgan sat up, throwing Tilson to the floor again. "What was that for?" She rubbed the ribs on her side where the tiny fey had poked her.

"That was for to get you out of bed, that's what that was for," Tilson grumbled as he picked himself off the floor. "What'cha still doing in bed, anyways? It's after midday, you know." He brushed the dust from his clothes and stood up straight. "Come on, get up already!"

"First of all," Morgan responded, "there's no school today so I get to sleep in as late as I want. Which is a pretty good thing, if you ask me, because I haven't been sleeping much lately.

"Second, we work at night. It's barely past noon, so you are waking me up way too early to be heading out. Third..." She looked over the edge of the bed, concerned. Tilson had been being awfully quiet, after all. Normally she wouldn't have even been able to get through her first point without being interrupted.

"Hey, that's mine! Leave it alone!" Morgan jumped out of bed and grabbed the packet of sketches that Tilson had discovered. Since her mother didn't approve of Morgan drawing in class or after school when she was supposed to be working on her homework, Morgan had kept them hidden in the bottom drawer of her dresser.

"Not like you could even tell what they were, anyways," the haltija sniffed. "That last one didn't even look anything like me."

"Of course it didn't look like you; it wasn't a

drawing of you at all. Why can't you keep your nose out of my things?" She stuffed the papers back into the drawer and covered them with an old sweatshirt before slamming the drawer closed again.

Tilson, meanwhile, had climbed back onto the bed and was standing on Morgan's pillow, his arms crossed and glaring. "You didn't have to knock me off the bed, you big oaf. Why do you have to do that every time I come to fetch you? I am only here because the council sent me to get you. You do remember the council, don't you?" The tiny fey stood and glared at her until Morgan had no choice but to back down.

Morgan just sighed. There was no reasoning with Tilson when his fur was in a bundle. She simply pulled open a different drawer and pulled out a pair of jeans. Listening to Tilson's ranting with only half an ear, she pulled out a shirt, socks and shoes. She took a glance at her clock again, trying to remember where her parents were. Normally, she would be able to hear them downstairs.

"It's still only barely past noon. Why does the council want us there so early?"

Tilson sputtered in indignation. "I...you...why you big...I knew it! You weren't even listening, were you?" He paced back and forth, leaving tiny indentations on the pillow before leaping to the ground. "Why do I even bother telling you anything if you won't even listen to what I am saying?" He walked across the floor to where the window was barely open. With a few quick steps, he bounded up and over the windowsill.

Downstairs, Morgan found a note from her parents. It was stuck to the refrigerator with a large magnet and explained that her mother had gone to a meeting and her father was out playing golf with his friends. Shaking her head, Morgan flopped the page over and scrawled a note back to them, explaining that she had gone down to the park for the afternoon. She had no idea how long she would be gone this time but it would at least be an excuse for her not being at the house if they got back before her.

Morgan caught up with Tilson at the edge of the trees and lifted him up onto Askel's back. She spent a couple minutes smoothing the soft feathers on Askel's neck, ignoring Tilson's muttering, before climbing up as well. She had no idea what had gotten Tilson's fur into such a knot; she just hoped it wasn't something that was going to come back down on her.

Askel flew them to the same island as before, but Morgan was able to get a much better view in the sunlight. A thick forest of trees covered the surface of Zea Island, with a pale ring of sand glowing under the clear green water that rippled and sparkled in the sunshine. As they got closer, Morgan was able to spot a school of large fish, barely under the surface of the water, dancing among the waves. Gentle ebbs of water broke onto the beach and teased at the trees before receding back into the river.

When they landed, Corran came forward to greet them as before. He bowed deeply to Morgan, Tilson and Askel before immediately leading them into the group of eagerly waiting fey. "Stormshock thinks he may have discovered a way of releasing the ether from the orbs."

He spoke not just to Morgan and her small band but to all of the council who were gathered there. A murmur came up from the crowd at his proclamation. Corran waved a hand for silence and waited for the fey to calm before continuing. "He has received word of a Master Smith, one who is reputedly able to craft anything."

He turned to face Morgan directly. "You must find him and ask him for a way of releasing the ether.

"There is one problem, however. Stormshock has not been able to discover exactly where this smith lives." He held up a calming hand as the fey began to murmur once more and raised his voice to be heard over the commotion. "He does know of one who may be able to help with that as well." He turned to face Morgan more fully. "You must speak with Amahté-Baki."

There was a gasp of surprise from the listening fey and not even Corran's raised hand was enough to silence the cacophony of murmuring this time. Morgan looked around at the council members who were whispering and debating among themselves, heads leaned towards each other to converse but none of them looking away from Morgan and Corran, to see if there would be more news.

Even steady, calm Askel, who had moved in closer to the group, seemed shaken by Corran's announcement. He was quietly snuffling and pawing at the ground. Morgan moved through the crowded fey to her friend and began to smooth the ruffled feathers on his neck.

When the council finally quieted down enough for her to ask, Morgan looked back to Corran. "Who is Amahté-Baki?"

"Amahté-Baki is one of the Ancients, the last one known to exist. Many doubt that he yet survives, but if Stormshock is willing to send you to meet with him, it must be true." Corran moved closer to the girl. "If this is true, and you are able to meet with him, you will be the first to do so in over a thousand years.

"Many of us have only heard the stories of the Ancients, legends that have been handed down from our elders. To think of actually meeting one is quite astounding." He reached out to take Morgan's unresisting hand. "Come. Stormshock is waiting."

The dragon was nestled in his pool, unable to be seen from the entrance of the glade, just as he had been the first time Morgan had been to see him. Upon Morgan's arrival through the wooded tunnel, however, Stormshock drew himself from the water to greet her.

One giant leap took the colossal green dragon across the winding path to land, surprisingly gracefully, by the trees before her. "I had hoped that you would spare no time in coming to see me, and I thank you for your swift arrival. I assume that Corran has told you of the journey I must now ask of you." Rivulets of water cascaded off of his body as he landed.

Morgan reflexively took a step back as the dragon hit the ground scant paces in front of her. She took a deep breath and nodded, but hesitantly. "Corran told me that I'm to meet with the Ancient, Amahté-Baki, but he didn't tell me very much beyond that." She took a second step backwards and a deep breath. "He said that just about everyone believed all of the Ancients were gone, since none of them have been seen in a long time."

The enormous dragon nodded. "That is true; most believe the Ancients to have long since passed into the ether, but we need you to go see the one that still lives. He has been sleeping for a great many years, so even we hadn't realized until very recently that he yet lives."

Morgan looked up to meet the dragon's eyes, far above her. "Where do I have to go?"

Stormshock led her to the pool in the center of the clearing, where he settled back down into the water. "It is a distance away, I must admit, but I must stress that it is a necessary journey. The Ancient is located on the other side of the world, in the country you humans refer to as Egypt."

Morgan stopped climbing halfway up the rocks and her eyes widened in astonishment. "Egypt? I can't go to Egypt! That's way too far away, and my parents would notice I was gone."

"Unfortunately, it is true that your disappearance would be noticed. However, I believe I may have a solution to that particular problem."

Morgan shook her head and moved down to her customary seat among the rocks. "I know that my parents are gone a lot and I can sneak off for a few hours here and there, but... to go all the way to Egypt? I'd have to be gone for more than one night. They would definitely notice I was missing."

"True." Stormshock settled further into the water. "Unless it was worked out so that your family was not aware that you were gone at all."

Morgan was confused. "How could they not know I was gone?"

The great dragon grinned. "Many of the fey have abilities far beyond those of humans. Some of us are even able to take the shape of another for short periods of time. I have discussed this with Liore, who is one capable of transforming herself as such, and she is willing to stand in your stead while you are away. She has performed such favors for us and other chosen in the past and has performed remarkably well.

"You will, of course, have to spend a bit of time with her, in order for her to fully master your shape, manner of speaking, and the like, but all in all, it should not be too difficult."

Morgan adjusted her seat on the section of rock and thought about this. "I suppose something like that could work. But how am I supposed to get to Egypt? Askel can't fly me that far, can he?"

"Well, yes, he could, but he will not be delivering you this time. I have other means of transporting you to where you need to be."

"So I'm going to be on my own?" She had gotten used to her companions and wasn't enthused about the idea of leaving them behind while she was on the other side of the world.

Stormshock chuckled. "I am sending the others with you as usual. While Askel will not be taking you there himself, he will be arriving shortly after you do. I have something that I need him to deliver along the way, so he should be only a few hours behind you."

Morgan exhaled in relief. Travelling halfway around the world to meet this Ancient sounded bad enough as it was, but Morgan would not have been as pleased about having to go alone. "Do they know yet?"

"They will soon. Do not worry yourself about it. Right now, I suggest you go speak with Corran. I believe he has some supplies already gathered for you. Liore will be by to see you after sundown tonight. Askel will be leaving shortly after he takes you home tonight, and you and Tilson will be leaving tomorrow night. Another will be coming to your house to get you, so be prepared."

Morgan headed back out of Stormshock's clearing, still in a daze from what she had been told. Egypt! She had never dreamed that she would be going there, although she had seen many pictures in books and seen bits and pieces on the television. She wandered out of the wooded tunnel and back into the council clearing.

Corran was still waiting by the entrance. Now he held a satchel that bulged with supplies. He also held out a leather-wrapped disk.

"What's this?" Morgan fingered the disk. It was round, almost an inch and a half across, deep green in color and slightly glossy in the light. It was engraved with a strange design consisting of a stylized teardrop shape and a lightning bolt. Although the disk was no thicker than a quarter, the etching seemed much deeper.

"It is Stormshock's symbol, to let Amahté-Baki know that you are his emissary," Corran explained. "One of Stormshock's own scales, etched with his rune. Only one who is allowed would dare to carry a symbol such as this. It is a high honor, indeed."

"Oh!" Morgan admired the scale for a moment longer before asking, "What's an emissary?"

"An emissary is a person who speaks on another's behalf. That scale will verify to the Ancient that you are the chosen one, sent by Stormshock."

That made sense, so Morgan rewrapped the strange-looking symbol in its protective leather and tucked it into her pocket before adjusting the strap of the satchel onto her shoulder to be more comfortable.

"Stormshock said that Askel wouldn't be coming to get me tomorrow night, that he was sending someone else to take me to see the Ancient. Do you know who is coming?"

"I believe he is planning to send Vouivre."

"Who is that?"

Corran chuckled. "You will see tomorrow. For now, it looks like your friends are ready to go." He gestured to where Tilson was already loaded onto Askel's back.

"Remember to dress warmly tomorrow

night. The Ancient may live in a desert, but it is not always so warm there. It still gets quite cold, and there is a decent amount of flying distance to think of as well."

Morgan thanked him and hefted the satchel onto her back again. The longer she wore the pack, the heavier it seemed to feel, but she didn't want to complain about it. She was sure that whatever was inside was necessary and she could always look through it all once she got back home.

That evening, Morgan took a look through the supplies in the pack that Corran had sent home with her. She wasn't sure what she had expected to find inside but there was plenty to look at. The first thing she pulled out was a small bag that was filled with some assorted dried meats, cheeses, fruits, crackers and nuts. Beneath the bag was a coil of soft, thin rope. Morgan pulled this out and stretched out a length of it, surprised by its lightness. The entire coil only weighed about as much as her shoes.

A light brown blanket was folded and rolled into a tight bundle at the bottom of the pack.

It was not the softest blanket that Morgan had ever felt, but it was not as coarse as the heavy wool blanket that her dad loved so much.

Tucked in next to the blanket was a leather-bound book. When Morgan opened it to see what it contained, she was surprised to see page after page of blank paper. Shrugging, she tucked it back into the pack.

In a pocket on the outside of the satchel she found a strange leather pouch that was wrapped tightly with a cord at one end. There was nothing inside but the leather felt like it had been worked until it was very thin and flexible. She put it back and decided to ask about it later.

Morgan tucked everything back into the satchel and added a couple things of her own. First of all, she put in the flashlight and a couple sets of extra batteries that she had gotten. Also, she added a couple of pens and a pencil with a good eraser. Just in case, she added a pack of matches that her parents would be upset to discover that she had found.

After thinking for a few minutes longer, she went to a drawer and pulled out the ring that

Tilson had given her when they went to the dragon's lair up in the frozen cold. Lastly, she put Stormshock's symbol into one of the smaller pockets, where she could get to it quickly if she needed to.

She closed up the pack and started to put it away, but changed her mind. Running downstairs, she took a handful of granola bars out of the box in the cupboard and brought them up to add to the collection. She stashed the satchel in her closet and put one of her jackets over the top of it. First, so that if her mother peeked into the closet, she wouldn't have any reason to ask where the pack came from, and second, to make sure that Morgan didn't forget her jacket again.

After all that was set to go, Morgan sat back to wait.

About an hour after sunset, as Morgan was stretched out on her bed busily turning notebook paper into a fleet of airplanes, Tilson crawled in through the window, followed by an elvor that Morgan had not yet met. The elvor looked much like Corran, with the same golden skin and silver hair, but this elvor was much shorter than Corran, and her hair was not as long. She was dressed in brown pants and a cream-colored shirt.

Once inside Morgan's room, she held out a hand. "Everyone calls me Liore. You must be Morgan."

Morgan nodded and shook the small elvor's hand. "You must be the one that I was told about, to take my place while I'm gone."

"Yep, that's me. I am the best at shifting, so I get to be all sorts of different people. Gotten pretty good at it too, if I do say so myself." Liore winked, still holding onto Morgan's hand.

As Morgan's eyes widened in shock, Liore began to glow softly. Her form became slightly blurred so that none of her features could be seen clearly. The glow got steadily brighter until Morgan had to shield her eyes from the brightness. Liore softly reached out her other hand to take Morgan's hands from her face. "I can't mimic what I can't see. I am almost done, just another minute."

Morgan dropped her hand and nodded, squinting against the blinding light. Thankfully, before too much more time had passed, the glow began to fade, and Morgan could see again. What she saw surprised her.

Standing before her, still holding onto one of her hands, stood a duplicate of herself, complete with clothing and a hole in the toe of her left sock. Morgan looked down at her toes and wiggled them, and watched as Liore did the same, in unison. She raised an arm and waved her hand, amused to see her reflection doing the same.

"Pretty good, I think. I know it's kind of weird to see yourself like this, so hang on, and I can change back." Liore let go of Morgan's hand and took a step backwards. "You can close your eyes this time but it will be much faster, I promise."

Soon, Liore was back in her own form. She explained to Morgan, "The next time I have to take your shape will be a lot easier because I already did it once. The first time with someone new is always the hardest and takes the longest. I have an easier time when I have physical contact but now that I have done it once, I can change into you anytime." She winked again and continued. "Even if you aren't here."

Morgan nodded and sat back onto her bed. "You do this a lot?"

"Oh, yeah, at least a couple times a month, for one reason or another. Mostly to cover for the chosen like you but sometimes just for fun," the fey shifter grinned. "It's always amusing watching humans when they find out that they were seen somewhere that they weren't at."

She sat on the bed next to Morgan. "But to truly pass for you while you are gone, I need to know more about you. You're in school, right?" At Morgan's nod, she continued. "What grade are you in? Looks like you would be in what, eighth?"

"Yeah, I'm in eighth grade."

"What classes are you taking? Any that you are having a hard time in, or ones that are pretty easy?"

Morgan looked at her in shock. "You're going to school for me too?"

"Well, yeah, you can't exactly take a lot of time off without people noticing. Don't worry; I've been to school plenty of times. What about friends? Got any of those that I need to know about? Boyfriend?"

When Morgan shook her head to all of the elvor's questions, Liore clucked in sympathy. "I kind of figured. Most of the people in your world are pretty lonely."

Morgan and Liore stayed up until early in the morning, talking about the different things going on in Morgan's life. Liore spent quite a bit of time imitating Morgan's voice and handwriting, looking at Morgan's homework papers to make sure that she would be able to pass herself off as her.

Finally, unable to stay awake any longer, Morgan fell asleep on her bed in the middle of a discussion over her daily routine. Unperturbed, Liore watched her sleep.

Morgan was drowsy through the next day in school but spent a long time making notes about the different things that Liore might need to know, like the math test coming up that she had to pass and the writing assignment on the life cycle of plants that needed to be turned in.

When she got home, although Tilson was nowhere to be seen, Liore was already there. She was playing one of Morgan's new video games and snacking on corn chips that she must have found downstairs. "I hadn't played this one before; it's pretty fun. Do you know if you have any Pepsi?"

That night, after saying goodnight to her parents and gathering up all the equipment that she would need for the journey, Morgan watched Liore take her shape once more and crawl into bed. Morgan snuck with her satchel and coat down the stairs and waited on the back porch, watching to see who was going to come get her.

After waiting for over an hour, after the moon was high in the sky, she started to think that she had misunderstood when she was supposed to be heading out to see the Ancient. Maybe she was to head out tomorrow, so of course nobody would come for her tonight. She thought back on exactly what Stormshock and Corran had each told her, wondering if she had been confused about something, but then noticed a shadowed form flying in from the distant clouds towards her.

The shape was enormous, a huge winged shape with a long tail drifting behind its massive body. Morgan took a step back, deeper into the shadows as it landed, hoping that this was the one sent by Stormshock and not an unwelcome visitor.

The enormous creature came into the field behind the house and landed in about the same area that Askel normally landed in. It was even bigger than Morgan had initially realized, not quite the size of a dragon but much, much larger than Askel. It was almost as tall as a single-story house and its tail stretched out behind it, just about the length of its body. It was covered in a dark brown hairless skin or some sort of leathery hide, Morgan couldn't tell which, and stood on two legs that ended in sharply clawed feet. Its bat-like wings were a lighter brown than the rest of its body and the creature tucked them in against its sides once it was settled onto the field.

After settling its wings down and moving its legs around to be steadier on the ground, the creature dipped its long neck low until its head almost touched the grass beneath it. A small form, made even smaller in comparison to the size of the larger creature it had been riding, slid down its neck and off its head, landing in a skittering run on the ground. Even at this distance, Morgan could recognize Tilson and relaxed.

Morgan stepped out of the shadows, picked up her satchel and headed out across the grass to meet up with Tilson and the strange flying creature. Tilson jumped up as soon as Morgan was in range, forcing Morgan to lean down and scoop him up before he crashed into her. She hefted the haltija, along with Tilson's tiny pack, onto her shoulder and slowed as she approached the massive, winged beast.

"What're you stalling for? Let's go!" Tilson grumbled as she hesitantly approached the creature.

The creature lifted its head until it was level with Morgan and looked at her with one crimson eye. After appraising her for a long moment, it opened a mouth, filled with rows of sharp, pointed teeth. "Are you ready to go? We have a long flight ahead of us."

Its voice was low and growly, more of a rumble deep in its throat than actual language. Surprised to hear the flying fey speak, Morgan stopped in her tracks. "You can talk!"

The creature let out a chuckle that sounded more like a growl. "Yes, I speak. Just about all of we fey are able to speak, but humans have forgotten many of our languages.

"In fact, I am able to speak three, one of which is close enough to pass as your own."

Still surprised, Morgan nodded and slung her heavy bag over the creature's back, looking for a way to climb up as well.

As soon as she was settled into place, the creature ducked its head, spread its considerable wings to either side, crouched low to the ground and sprung into the air, thrusting its wings downward at the same time. The leap, combined with the wings' force, shot them straight into the air much faster than Morgan had been expecting. Unable to find a good hold on the creature's back, she leaned forward and wrapped her arms about its neck, hanging on for all she was worth.

After gaining enough altitude to fly safely, the creature turned its head back on its impossibly long neck to look at Morgan. "Are you all right? There truly is no reason to be afraid. I will not drop you."

Morgan nodded, keeping her head turned to the side to take a deep breath. The creature had almost no scent, at least not any that Morgan could detect. While not warm, its hide was not overly cool, either.

"I'm OK," she responded. "I just wasn't used to taking off that fast."

The creature chuckled, a strange hissing noise. "Ah, yes. You are much more used to riding the gryphon, aren't you?"

Morgan nodded. "I was told your name, but I can't remember what it was. You're the one that Corran told me about, aren't you?"

"I am. My name is Vouivre, and it's my job to ensure that you are brought safely to the Ancient, and to bring you home once more after you are finished."

"How long do you suppose it'll take us to get there?" Morgan knew that Egypt was a long distance off and she hoped that the flight wouldn't wear Vouivre out too much. She wasn't looking forward to the idea of having to settle down to make camp partway there.

"We should be there shortly after sunup.

Have no worries, for I have made journeys far longer than this in the past."

The wind blowing past them from the speed that they were flying made talking difficult, so Morgan settled down to watch the scenery fly past, much more swiftly than she had ever flown before. Soon, however, the lateness of the hour and the sheer exhaustion of all the excitement wore her down, and she drifted off to sleep, nestled comfortably between Vouivre's beating wings.

Her last thought as she drifted off was one of amusement, for she had apparently gotten into the habit of sleeping during these flights, so she really hoped that she never learned how to fly; she just might end up falling asleep high in the air.

~ 8 ~

AMAHTÉ-BAKI

They flew through the night and Morgan soon woke to the dry, stifling heat over the desert sands. Looking down over the side of Vouivre's massive body, she could see nothing but gentle hill-like mounds of pale golden sand stretching around below her.

Soon the desert gave way to barren plains, where Morgan could see grasses and small shrubs fighting to grow through the cracked earth. At the furthest edge of her vision, gigantic structures rose above the horizon.

As the small group approached, Morgan could finally recognize the familiar shape of the pyramids. Larger and larger they grew until Morgan could only gape in amazement at their sheer size. Seeing the famous pyramids on the television didn't really prepare her for seeing one in person, where even in flight they loomed over her. Somehow, she hadn't expected them to be so *big*.

Finally, Vouivre landed in the sand beyond the largest of the pyramids. In the distance, Morgan could see another of the well-known icons of the Egyptian desert. Amid tall walls of stone the same pale tan color of the desert sands, the legendary sphinx watched silently over the quiet morning. It was also larger than Morgan had expected, even though she was not close enough to tell how tall it actually was.

Tilson shook himself fully awake; he had taken to sleeping during the flights as well. Climbing up Vouivre's neck, he looked around them to see any signs of life. Nothing stirred. The wind blew slightly, sending small drifts of sand over everything.

Morgan slid down from her perch as well and looked around. "Is someone supposed to meet us here, or do we have to go find the Ancient ourselves?"

After depositing Tilson onto the sand at Morgan's feet, Vouivre looked off into the distance. "Amahté-Baki is over there; we just have to approach. I am certain he is already aware of our arrival."

Morgan looked in the direction that Vouivre indicated. All she could see was the silent statue of the sphinx and miles upon miles of empty desert beyond. With a sigh, she pulled down her satchel and began to walk. She wasn't looking forward to trudging through the desert, but if that was what she had to do, so be it.

Tilson grabbed a hold of Morgan's pant leg and climbed up until he was riding on her shoulder. Vouivre followed a short distance behind, keeping a watchful eye around them as they went. The endless sand around them distorted things, making shapes appear in the rising sun, and the movement of time seemed to stop altogether. Morgan was soon thankful that Tilson had explained the strange leather item in her satchel, which was meant to carry water, so scarce in this hot environment.

When they neared the pyramids, Morgan stopped. People were walking around, digging in the sand and moving heavy machines around. "Wait, there are people here? How are we supposed to do this without getting caught, or showing everyone where the Ancient is?"

"You really don't listen, you know that? Such a human." Tilson looked over at Morgan. "You forget what you've been told as soon as you hear it, you know that?"

"What are you talking about?"

Tilson put his tiny paws on his hips and glared at Morgan, his tail swishing behind him. "They can't see us because we are fey and hidden by fey magic. Since you are here with us and you are the chosen, you are protected by the same magic. You could walk right up to one of them and stand in front of him and he still wouldn't see you there."

Morgan shook her head. "The same magic that lets us fly without being noticed. I forgot." She looked over at a group of workers and waved an arm at them, but none reacted. "Okay. Let's keep going." Ignoring the haltija's snort of derision, she made sure that he was secure on her shoulder as they continued.

As they passed the sphinx and the pair of crumbling buildings in front of it, however, Vouivre slowed. "The Ancient is in here."

Morgan looked around. "In where?" All she could see was sand upon sand upon more sand.

"Beneath the sands. He has been buried for a very long time." Vouivre stepped past Morgan and Tilson. "Stand back."

Morgan reached up to catch a better hold of the haltija and stepped a few paces away from Vouivre. Unsure as to what the giant creature was about to do, she turned partially away and looked to where the sphinx looked out over the desert.

A loud sound, one that Morgan recognized as being a heavy buffet from Vouivre's massive wings, caused her to turn back again. Morgan took a few steps further away and watched as Vouivre used his enormous wings to blow the sand away from them. She watched, fascinated, as the sand sprayed outwards in wall after wall.

Soon, Morgan could see something solid, now only marginally covered by the loose sand.

As Vouivre drove more sand away, Morgan could see some sort of stone buried beneath them. "What's that?"

"It is the residence of Amahté-Baki. He has remained hidden here, underground, for a very long time."

Morgan looked over at the group of workers who were not too far in the distance. A few of them were yelling and pointing at their direction. "I thought you said they couldn't see us? They're looking right at us!"

"They are not looking at us; they are looking at the sand. Since the sand is natural, it is not hidden by our magic. I assume their concern is because they have noticed it is moving."

Morgan watched as the workers yelled back and forth at each other, moving around to cover their work area with large cloths. "What are they doing?"

"Preserving their site," Vouivre replied. "They believe that a sandstorm is about to hit."

As she thought about it, the idea made sense to Morgan. "Like in Cinderflare's lair, where humans thought it was an eruption but it was really the dragon."

Before Morgan could ask anything further, a geyser of sand erupted at Vouivre's feet. Morgan started forward, but she was blinded by the hot spray. She yelped and fell a couple steps backward, trying to maintain her footing on the slippery ground.

Tilson shrieked and buried himself in the neck of Morgan's shirt, hiding his face from the stinging heat.

After a moment, the air cleared as the sand settled back down again, and Morgan could see a strange new creature had appeared. It appeared to be half man-shaped, but only from the waist up. From the waist down, it appeared to be some sort of bird, standing on taloned feet, much like Vouivre's. A long, thick tail rose up behind it, curving up over its back and ending in a sharp stinger.

When it turned to face Morgan, she could see that it was indeed human-headed, with darkly tanned skin and an even darker brown beard that grew down over its chest. The feathers over the bird-shaped lower half of the creature were the same dark brown as its beard, with feathers the color of chocolate ice cream on the underside. Its tail was also deep brown, much darker than the feathers, and ridges divided it into sections, almost like the tail of a scorpion.

Vouivre cried in alarm, "Stay back! Do not come close." He turned to face the repulsive creature and moved to put himself between it and Morgan. Spreading his great wings, he buffeted the monster.

The strange hybrid creature spread its large wings as well and took to the air, using the powerful gust from Vouivre's wings to lift itself high above the group. It dove at Morgan and extended the sharp spike at the end of its tail.

Vouivre dove directly into its path, using his wings and powerful legs to lift him airborne as well. He aimed directly towards the attacker, causing it to dive out of the way in order to not be hit. Vouivre quickly propelled himself higher than the man-bird beast and dove, issuing a high screech as he extended his claws to rake the beast from the air.

The beast, still dodging from Vouivre's initial move, darted impossibly fast to the side, narrowly missing Vouivre's attack. Noiselessly, it circled around to come up behind Vouivre, once more extending its horribly spiked tail to strike.

Much larger than the other beast, Vouivre was more powerful but not nearly as agile. He ducked to his left to try and avoid the lethal spike, but the beast managed to score a grazing hit. Vouivre screeched in pain as the beast grinned, already sensing its impending victory.

The strange creature pressed the advantage, following Vouivre as he dove, travelling faster and faster as he chased the giant to the ground. Its stinger darted forward once more, trying to attain a more direct hit into Vouivre's back.

Vouivre raised his wings high and used their immense strength to pull himself out of the dive, curving back upwards only inches from the ground.

The other creature hadn't been aware of how close the fighting pair had come to the sand. Because it had moved in to strike, it hadn't been able to see the ground rising up closer and closer. When Vouivre pulled out of the dive, its stinger missed Vouivre's back completely and buried deep into the sand. The beast landed hard and Morgan could hear the crunch of impact from her hiding spot a number of yards away.

Vouivre circled around quickly, keeping a close eye on the strange, aggressive beast as it began to push itself out of the sand. Much higher than before, Vouivre started into another dive, aiming directly for the beast.

Buried in the sand as it was, the creature was not able to get out of the way in time, although it changed tactics and instead tried to skitter beneath the sand to escape.

Vouivre made no sound as he plummeted, keeping his wings tucked in close to his massive body. Just as it appeared that Vouivre was about to crash into the sand as well, Morgan turned away, not wanting to see the impact. But instead of hearing another bone-crunching thud, there was only a keening wail, which quickly began to fade.

Morgan peeked back towards the battle, only to discover that she and Tilson were alone. Both the man-headed beast and Vouivre had disappeared. All that was left was the hole that Vouivre had made, with the blocks of stone buried beneath.

Morgan covered her eyes to block out the blinding sun and looked around the sky, but there was no sign of Vouivre. She looked down at Tilson. "I hope he's coming back."

The haltija peeked out from his hiding place in Morgan's shirt and looked around. "Where'd everybody go?"

Morgan shrugged and looked back at the stone, still mostly buried beneath the sand. "I have no idea; I wasn't looking. I think we're supposed to dig, though. Vouivre said that the Ancient was buried down there. I'm sure he'll be back."

She scanned the horizon one last time before turning back to the hole in the sand. "I hope."

Morgan and Tilson dug through the sand for a while, sweating both from the exertion and from the blistering sun. Finally, a shadow fell over the pair and Morgan looked up.

"He's back!"

The pair scrambled from the hole that they had only marginally been able to enlarge and ran towards their friend. Vouivre landed nearby and settled his wings back against his body. He walked quite calmly towards Morgan and Tilson.

"Are you all right?" Morgan asked.

Vouivre nodded and looked over at their progress. "We must hurry. The guardian will return soon, and we must be gone from here when he does."

"Return?" Morgan was confused. "Where is he?" Morgan had been entertaining ideas about Vouivre off eating the strange beast, or possibly taking it over the ocean to see if it would be able to swim its way back to the desert. The idea that it could already be on its way back to harass them before Morgan even had a chance to meet with the Ancient bothered her.

Vouivre walked towards the hole, grinning and showing far too many of his sharp, pointed teeth. "He needed to cool off, so I deposited him into the river. But it looked as though one of his wings had been broken so I believe he will have to walk back."

"So you knew that thing was going to be there?"

"I did. As I told you, my job was to get you to the Ancient safely. There was no way that the pair of you would be able to defeat the Ghirtablili."

"But why didn't you just kill it?" Morgan asked.

"The Ghirtablili is a rare type of guardian, one that cannot be killed easily. Even I would be hard-pressed to send that one into the ether."

Now that Vouivre was back, progress was much swifter on the opening to the Ancient's lair. By sundown, he had managed to uncover the crumbling ruins of what had once been an enormous statue.

It was shaped much like the sphinx, but most of the identifying features had long since eroded away. What was left was no more than heaps of limestone rocks in a somewhat animalistic shape. There was a vaguely feline body with no head and the remnants of one of its front paws, cracked and broken with age.

Vouivre seemed to become a bit more excited when they reached the paws in their digging. He sped up the pace of his wing buffets and even moved in closer to scratch at the sand with his claws to loosen up the hard-packed patches of sand close in to the rocks. Soon, there was a clear area where the group could walk up to the statue and stand between its paws.

Against the body, at what was now ground-level, the group could see a huge stone slab, which could only be there to block an entrance into the belly of the enormous statue.

Vouivre walked up close to the statue and reached out with one of his taloned feet to grasp at the stone. With a growl and an obvious amount of exertion, he shoved the stone aside.

It moved with a low grating noise which echoed into the dark silence within. The fading sun sent its rays beyond them into the opening, lighting up a long, steep tunnel that led down further underground. Vouivre stepped back to allow the others to enter.

"Are you sure?" Morgan looked back and up at Vouivre. When the large creature nodded, Morgan looked towards the doorway once more. "We have to go inside there?"

"Yes. The Ancient resides within. We must go to him." Vouivre took a step closer to the opening, which caused Morgan to start moving once more as well.

The sun was lowering towards the horizon and sweat beaded on Morgan's forehead as she moved into the relatively cooler shade of the statue. Thankfully, as they approached the opening, the air that was coming out of the opening was nowhere near as hot as the desert outside. They could all feel the temperature drop as they walked up to the doorway. Morgan breathed an audible sigh of relief, recalling how it had been hotter inside Cinderflare's cave than the air outside had been.

Once inside, all of them breathed a sigh of relief to be out of the stifling desert sun. The opening allowed barely enough light for them to navigate by but the thick stone blocked out most of the scorching heat. The floor was the same rough, cool limestone as the walls and ceiling, with barely any sand blown in from the mild breeze outside.

Deeper into the cavern, the light from the sun was not as bright so Morgan pulled out her flashlight, thankful that she had remembered to pack it. As the beam played over the walls, it revealed strange markings carved into the stone all around them, which continued down the length of the hall, leading straight to a large open room that they could now see ahead of them.

Carefully, the group stepped into the main chamber of the underground complex, looking around in awe at how much larger it was than any of them had expected. The great room was T-shaped, with arms heading off to the left and right, further than the flashlight could illuminate, with the main body of the room stretching out before them.

The walls were no longer bare stone but were now golden, as though someone had hammered pure gold onto the walls. There were still carvings etched in the gold but many of them now had inlays of other precious metals such as silver and bronze and many precious stones were placed both as part of the decoration and as pieces of the murals.

Morgan stepped closer to one of the walls next to her to have a better look. The etchings showed a number of reddish-brown-skinned and black-haired men, dressed in white skirts tied at the waist, but many of the men looked different than she had expected. As she perused these differences, Morgan noticed that a great many of the men were not men at all. Some were elvor, like Corran, and there were others that were short and stocky as Einar, and yet more that were even less human.

As she walked down the length of the mural, Morgan noticed that all of the figures seemed to be heading in the same direction that she was, as though they were all heading here to meet with the Ancient as well. A number of the carved figures were carrying baskets, boxes and other things, and Morgan wondered if she should have brought something, too.

Deeper into the room, statues loomed over them. The walls on both sides of the hall were lined with carved people, elvor, gryphons, and all sorts of different humans and fey. They were all carved much larger than life, most of them standing easily double Morgan's height. As she passed them, Morgan had the creepy feeling of being watched.

At the end of the hall of statues, the group encountered another door, this one too small for Vouivre to pass through. "I will remain here. The Ancient waits beyond." Vouivre took a few steps back and settled down on his haunches, keeping a watchful eye on the room around him, almost as though he expected the statues and the figures in the murals to come to life.

Tilson tried to stay behind with Vouivre, but he was overruled when Vouivre grabbed him in one claw and tossed him towards the door, where Morgan stood. "Quit being such a coward. You embarrass the name you bear."

Tilson rolled to a stop against the door and sputtered, glaring at Vouivre. He stood and brushed the dirt from his fur before walking over to Morgan and climbing up to her shoulder, still grumbling.

Morgan nodded and took a deep breath. Before entering the next chamber, she took off her pack and dug through it for a few moments, finally bringing forth the scale that Stormshock had sent with her. If Vouivre was right and the Ancient was in the room past this door, Morgan would need the identifying symbol soon.

The door was heavy and made of solid stone but Morgan was able to put her shoulder into it and heave it open enough to squeeze through. It made a mild scraping, grating noise as it moved, which echoed through the still room.

She couldn't help but think back to the cartoons she had watched as a young child. Every time the pyramids or the sphinx was depicted, there had been a mummy. The bandaged, undead monster had chased the heroes and sought revenge upon any who disturbed it. Even though she and her friends hadn't disturbed a tomb, weren't even in a pyramid, she couldn't help but feel apprehension about what she would be revealed beyond the heavy door.

Taking another deep breath, Morgan passed through the opening.

The room was much smaller than the last one had been, with lower ceilings. Its walls were decorated in precious metals and minerals as well. There were other objects in the room, also, such as the thick silk-covered pillows that were scattered throughout the room. There was a brazier at the end of the room with a low fire burning, and the smoke was pungent enough to make Morgan's eyes water and Tilson sneeze.

At the end of the chamber, another statue sat on a mound of thick pillows, bathed in the soft light of the fire from the brazier. It was catlike, with beautifully shaped golden fur, but its head had the features of a beautiful human woman. It had wings of pale gold, the same as its fur, and hair cascading down over its chest in the same hue. As Morgan walked up to it, she realized that this was no statue.

Statues don't breathe.

Morgan stopped moving, frozen in place. The creature was easily eight feet tall seated; Morgan couldn't even imagine how tall she would be if she stood up, especially if she stood on her hind legs.

Hesitantly, she took the last few steps to approach the creature, holding Stormshock's symbol before her like a shield.

The golden creature slowly opened its impossibly bright green eyes and looked at Morgan. "My greetings, emissary of the Council. I have been waiting for you." Her eyes seemed to glow on their own, even without the light from either Morgan's flashlight or the fire that was burning in the brazier. Her voice was soft and smooth, coming out almost as a purr.

Morgan blinked. "Are you Amahté-Baki?"

"I am."

Morgan held out Stormshock's scale so that the Ancient could see it better. "I was sent to ask of you the location of the Master Smith, the one who may be able to release the trapped dragons."

"Of course. I do know of the one to whom you are referring, and I will tell you." She blinked and turned her head to look at her more fully. "If you can answer my question. Be aware, however, that if you answer incorrectly, or if you do not answer at all, your life will be forfeit."

Morgan's eyes widened and she took a step back. "What...what do you mean forfeit?"

"If you are unable to answer my question correctly, I will have you for my next meal. Is this understood?"

Tilson whimpered on her shoulder, and Morgan took another step backwards before she realized what she was doing. When she noticed that she was backing up, she forced herself to stop moving. "How long will I have to answer?"

"Since you are an emissary of the council, I will grant to you two sunsets from tonight. But if you have not returned by then, I will come find you."

Morgan could feel the blood sinking to her feet, and she wondered how long she would be able to remain upright. When she had agreed to come out here to talk to the Ancient, she had not anticipated that she might not survive the conversation. Now she wasn't sure what to do. She wanted to get the answer to bring back to the council, for she had already started to consider a number of the fey that she had met as friends. On the other hand, she really didn't want to become lunch for Amahté-Baki.

After a few moments spent debating with herself, Morgan agreed.

"Rivers without water;
Forests without trees;
Mountains without rocks;
Towns without people;
What am I?"

~ 9 ~

RIDDLE

Morgan and Tilson retreated from the lair of the Ancient and met back up with Vouivre, wasting no time in exiting back out into the desert. Once outside and into the open once more, Morgan looked around for the Ghirtablili, surprised that it was nowhere to be seen. She quickly dropped the satchel into the sand and dug through it, looking for the book of blank paper that Corran had packed into it.

Apparently, this was what it was for.

She wrote the Ancient's strange riddle down, leaving a bit of room at the bottom of the page to make notes as she debated over the answer.

She hoped that she would be able to come up with the correct answer for it. Morgan really didn't like the idea of becoming anyone's lunch.

The hot desert sun had long since set and she shivered in the cold wind. Now that there was no longer the blistering heat beating down on them, the breeze that had seemed so mild through the day was much less comforting.

Tilson was shivering, too, huddling inside Morgan's shirt to keep warm. Vouivre stepped up close to them to block as much of the wind as he could, but it was little help.

"We need to find someplace warm to stay," Tilson chattered. "We won't make it out here for too long like this."

For once, Morgan agreed with the haltija. She looked around, but all she was able to see were miles and miles of sand-filled desert and crumbling ruins. "But where?"

"Follow me." Tilson took off across the sand, heading directly for one of the excavation sites set up next to a pyramid. Morgan followed, thinking that the haltija had spotted a tent that they could borrow for a night, but that was not the case. Tilson bypassed all of the excavating machinery and supplies, heading instead for the entrance that the excavation crew had propped open that led directly into the pyramid.

"No, wait! We can't go in there!" Morgan tried to catch up to her scurrying friend, but Tilson had too much of a lead. When Tilson disappeared down the entrance tunnel, Morgan had no choice but to follow.

"There are people digging in here. Even if we can't be seen, they're going to notice that there's something wrong!"

Tilson ignored her protests and headed deeper into the pyramid.

The corridor was cool, not as cold as the night outside, but definitely not as hot as it had been throughout the day. The stone flooring underfoot had been cleared of most of the sand, but there were still loose patches here and there that the group had to be watchful for. The ceiling was high enough that Vouivre was able to stoop down low enough to follow, but there wasn't a lot of room for maneuvering once they were all inside the tunnel.

The passageway sloped downwards at a gentle angle, finally ending at a pair of old, bronze doors. An inscription had long ago been etched into the doors, written in a language that Morgan couldn't read:

maut beebe ta tkour tnx ern laps w0 pai 0fw ashr wrro

Morgan paused at the doors, looking at the inscription. Although she couldn't understand what the words meant, wasn't sure that she was even seeing all of the words because they were so old and worn, she was certain that they were not words of welcome. She had heard of all sorts of bad things happening to people who entered the pyramids, stories about curses and mummies.

She was pretty sure that she had seen this type of warning in a movie or three.

It never turned out well.

Tilson wasn't nearly as worried as Morgan about the strange inscription. He went up to the doors and began to push on them in the vain hope that he could open them. "Come on, give me a hand here!"

"Maybe this isn't such a good idea."

Tilson looked back up at her. "You're right; maybe it's not. Maybe we should just go back outside and freeze to death. While we're at it, why don't we just hold out a welcome sign and wait for that guardian to get back; I am sure he'll be happy to see us. That's a much better idea, don'tcha think?" He put his hands on his hips and stared up at Morgan indignantly.

Morgan sighed. There was no arguing with Tilson when the haltija was in a mood, so even trying was pointless. She stepped closer to the door, trying not to step on the tiny fey, and pushed.

The heavy bronze door swung open a lot more easily than Morgan had expected it to, causing her to stumble a bit as it opened. She grabbed the door for support as she went, barely avoiding a tumble down the steep flight of stairs that were immediately through the doorway.

Once Morgan regained her footing and was no longer in any danger of falling forward, Tilson headed off to see where the stairs led. Vouivre moved carefully along behind Morgan as he followed Tilson, placing his talons gingerly to avoid a fall himself.

The stairs led down a short distance, about

one and a half floors in Morgan's estimation. At the bottom, they found a small landing and another set of gigantic doors, these made of thick stone. A few feet before the doors sat a large chest, also made of stone and carved much like the huge bronze doors had been, with similar strange lettering. A pair of statues stood guard on either side of the chest.

The statues were small, only about two feet taller than Morgan. They were not made of stone like the doors and chest, as Morgan had initially thought, but rather of some sort of clay. They were shaped mostly like humans, with huge, barrel-shaped chests and arms that hung down to their knees. Clothing had been carved onto them, in the same strange skirts as the ones in the Ancient's lair had been.

The stone box, on closer inspection, was not made entirely of stone, either. Tilson had managed to pick off part of the stone that was attached to the cover, revealing a wooden substance beneath. Morgan moved closer to have a better look but refrained from touching the box, afraid of what may be inside. Although it was not nearly large enough to hold a coffin, only being a couple feet across and a foot or so wide, Morgan still didn't want to open it to find anything icky inside.

The doors, however, were made of stone. Unlike the previous set of doors, these were without inscription, apparently deliberately left blank. Since they couldn't make camp on a flight of stairs and needed to go further into the complex, Morgan leaned against the doors and gave an experimental push.

The doors refused to budge. Even when Morgan pushed with all her might, she was unable to get them to move in the slightest.

"I guess we'll have to make do here." Morgan looked around at the narrow ledge and flight of stairs, wondering how they would all be able to get any rest whatsoever.

Even more than that, she was curious to see what was further inside the structure. If she had to worry about the curse of a mummy, it was too late to change what had already happened. She knew that there was almost no chance that she would ever get to see inside a pyramid again and she wanted to see just a little bit more of it before they had to stop.

"Allow me to pass. I may be able to open them." Vouivre moved as close to one of the side walls as he could, giving enough room for Morgan and Tilson to skitter behind him, up a number of stairs.

Vouivre tucked his wings in even tighter against his body and leaned into one of the doors. With a grunt of exertion, he pressed with his legs. Finally, there was a loud grating sound and the doors slowly slid open enough to pass through.

After making sure that the doors wouldn't swing back shut again. Vouivre stepped aside once more and let Morgan and Tilson enter first.

A long hall stretched out before them, much further than Morgan's flashlight could illuminate. She entered cautiously, sweeping the light before them. The hall was about twice the length of Morgan's house, and almost as wide. There were markings on the wall and old, faded and peeling paintings of some strange bird-headed man.

At the far end of the hall, another set of

stone doors stood, flanked by another pair of clay statues.

"I believe that it is best we rest here for the night," Vouivre said.

The others agreed, so they moved back to the midpoint of the hall and settled down. Vouivre, exhausted, settled down much like a bird would. He wrapped his leathery wings about himself and tucked his feet beneath his body. Morgan pulled the blanket out of her satchel and wrapped it around herself. Tilson climbed in with her, and the pair of them settled down next to Vouivre.

As they settled down, Morgan took one last look around her, amazed that they had come this far into one of the pyramids, just a little disappointed that she couldn't even tell anyone about it.

In the morning, Morgan shared some of the dried foods that Corran had given her and repacked the satchel, making sure that everything was ready to go. When Morgan asked about the Ghirtablili, concerned that it might attack them again when they left the pyramid, Vouivre calmed her fears.

"His job is to stop anyone from entering the Ancient's lair. Since we are not trying to get back inside, he will not bother with us."

"Even though you took him off and dropped him into a river?"

Vouivre nodded, so Morgan decided to trust him. She picked up her satchel and hitched the strap up onto its customary position on her shoulder.

Morgan had not slept well that night, worrying over the Ghirtablili, being eaten by Amahté-Baki, and whether the group would be able to solve the strange riddle. As the group headed back out of the tunnels below the pyramid, she mused to herself. "What is a river without water? Or a forest without trees?" Climbing back up the steps that led to the sands outside, she rolled ideas around in her head, trying to puzzle out the answer. "A river without water would be dried up, like an arroyo. A forest without trees would just be regular land, though. A meadow? A field? There wouldn't be water or trees there."

She was still musing as they entered the bright sunlight of the desert morning. She held up a hand against the glare and looked around, half expecting to see the Ancient demanding an answer already.

What she saw, however, was a gryphon trotting towards them.

"Askel!" Morgan ran to her friend and wrapped her arms around the gryphon's neck, burying her face in his soft feathers. "We missed you!"

Askel stretched his neck around to nuzzle the girl, careful to not scratch her with his sharp beak.

After a brief reunion, Morgan began explaining about the riddle that the Ancient had given her and the consequence of answering incorrectly. She pulled out the book where she had scrawled the lines of the puzzle and showed them to Askel.

"I was thinking maybe some sort of meadow or field, but that wouldn't answer the part about the mountain without rocks, or the city without people." She looked back at the notes she had made once more. "I have to answer this right, or she's going to eat me. I don't want to be food."

Askel nodded, not in agreement, but with understanding and looked back at the riddle in Morgan's book once more.

Vouivre and Tilson came over as well and they all moved over to a pile of stones that was heaped in the shade not too far from the entrance to Amahté-Baki's lair. Vouivre agreed that the stones were not close enough to the Ancient's lair that the guardian would see them as being a threat. There, they all sat and huddled together, trying to think of possible answers.

"Maybe it's a ghost town," Tilson suggested. "That's a town without people."

Morgan shrugged. "But that only answers a part of the riddle. A forest without trees wouldn't be a ghost town; neither would a river without water."

"Maybe it's a ghost town near a dried river. Could that be it?" Vouivre asked. "Maybe the answer is a specific area or place."

Morgan perked up a bit at this. "Hey, yeah! Maybe we just need to figure out where there's an abandoned town with a dry river near it or something."

"But what about the mountain?" Tilson asked. "There's no such thing as a mountain without rocks."

Morgan slumped again. "Yeah." She thought about this for a few minutes. "Maybe it's a mountain of dirt? Or something in it other than rocks?"

"Like crystal, or gems or something." Tilson's eyes widened. "Maybe there's a whole mountain out there that's just stuffed full of gems and gold!" He stood up on the rock and began pacing back and forth. "Can you imagine a whole mountain full of gold? We'd all be rich, richer than rich!"

"I doubt that's it," Vouivre stated. "There isn't much chance that the Ancient would be asking about a mountain of gold. She hasn't much use for that."

"Maybe it's something else entirely," Morgan mused. "Maybe it doesn't really have much to do with the pieces as they are; maybe it's something about the words themselves, not what they mean."

Everyone looked confused, so Morgan opened the book once more and looked at the writing in it. "Maybe the letters spell out something completely different." She turned to a blank page and pulled out her pencil. When everyone still looked at her confused, she started to spell out the words. "Like the letters of 'rivers' without the letters of 'water,' so that would leave... r, i, v, and s." She wrote the four letters onto the paper and turned back to the riddle. "Forests, without the letters in 'trees' would leave an f and an o." She wrote these down with the previous letters. "Mountains without rocks would leave m, u, n, t, a, i, and another n. Finally, 'towns without people' leaves t, w, n, and s."

She sat back and looked at the grouping of letters, trying to fit them into an answer that would satisfy the Ancient. Thinking back to the many games of Scrabble she had played at home, she pulled out a piece of paper and tore it into small squares, writing a letter on each piece so that she could move them around to form new words.

"If most turn in swan...That leaves a v." She rearranged the letters again. "Of man's wits...That leaves a lot of letters too."

Many times over the next couple hours, Morgan thought she had hit on something only to run out of letters, or need more that she didn't have. The others got into the spirit of things, too, making suggestions and moving pieces around to make new words. Eventually, however, Morgan had to give up. "I just don't think that's the answer."

The sun was high overhead by then and their comfortable shade had moved on, leaving all of them feeling more than a little overheated, so they decided to move back into the coolness of the pyramid tunnels. They had to sneak past the workers, who had returned to their digging site now that the sandstorm was over. This proved to be remarkably easy, as the group simply walked among the humans, completely unnoticed.

Oddly, every now and again one of the workers would actually move out of the way of the group as they passed, seeming to give them enough space to move around them without appearing to realize what they were doing. Morgan followed, still mulling over the riddle in her head. Amahté-Baki had only given her until tomorrow night to solve it and Morgan could feel the time slipping away. Her time was almost gone. If she couldn't figure out the answer, she would only have hours left to live.

When night fell, Morgan gathered up some wood from the excavation site outside and used the matches that she had brought to light a small fire in the middle of the hall that they had made camp in the previous night. She pulled out her blanket and snuggled down against Askel, both for warmth and for the small amount of comfort from having her friend there.

Morgan wasn't expecting to sleep very well that night but she was a lot more tired than she had expected, not having slept much the night before. She drifted off to sleep almost immediately, with her friends all curled up nearby. As she slipped into slumber, Morgan felt Tilson crawl under the covers to sleep as well.

When she woke in the morning, she still hadn't come up with any answers to the riddle. "So much for the mind working on your problems in your sleep," she muttered to herself. "Come on, Tilson, its morning." She peeked under the covers to Tilson's usual spot, but the haltija was already gone.

"Now what's he up to?" Morgan wondered as she put her blanket away. Anytime Tilson wandered off on his own, it usually caused more problems for his friends. Morgan wasn't sure how many more problems she could deal with today.

As she packed everything away in preparation for another long day of mental exercises in the sun, Morgan kept an eye out for the haltija. Just as Morgan tucked away the last of the supplies and was about to go looking for him, Tilson appeared from the side passage that led off the main cavern.

"Oh, you're up," Tilson said when he noticed Morgan. "I was just starting to wonder if you were planning to sleep all day. You humans can be so lazy."

"I've been up for a while, wondering where you were," Morgan answered as she slung the pack over her shoulder, refusing to be drawn into another argument with the tiny fey. "Where were you, anyways?"

"Exploring. You can't expect me to just sit

around and watch you sleep, can you?" Tilson climbed up onto Askel's back and got comfortable, leaning back against his little pack.

Although Tilson was looking much too proud of himself, Morgan wasn't going to ask what he had done. Whatever it was, Morgan was sure that she would find out later, probably the hard way. She adjusted the weight of her satchel on her back and headed down the tunnel towards the entrance leading outside.

The sun was every bit as searing outside as it had been the previous day. Rather than just sitting at the group of rocks that they had used earlier, Vouivre and Askel dragged the stones over to a bigger shaded area so that they could be cooler for a longer period of time. Without much breeze, it wasn't great, but it was better.

Morgan pulled out her notebook again and began to read through the passages, hoping to notice something that would direct her towards an answer. She sighed. They were running out of time.

After she sat for a couple hours musing and coming up with idea after idea, none of which could have been correct, the breeze picked up a bit, a welcome relief from the afternoon heat. Morgan rolled up the sleeves of her shirt to let the wind cool her a little bit more and Tilson stood and turned to face the breeze, holding out his arms and leaning slightly into the wind. Even Askel and Vouivre shook out their wings to catch some of the cooler air.

The wind didn't last long but the group was in a bit higher spirit for it. Everyone sat back down at the rocks and Morgan picked up a stick that had blown towards them. She settled down in the sand and used the rock as a back rest, absently doodling on the ground with the stick.

"Rivers." She drew a couple of wavy lines, not even worrying too much about making them look like rivers. "Forests." She drew some puffy, lumpy circles, like the tops of trees that she had drawn when she was much younger. "Mountains." She added some upside-down Vs, a bunch of them all grouped together. "And towns." She drew in a few Xs as well.

Sighing, she looked at it all put together. "Well, that doesn't help much."

Askel looked down at what the girl was talking about and snorted in surprise. He stood up and pawed at the ground, around Morgan's scratching.

Tilson stood up too. "I think he's saying you are onto something." He moved closer to see more clearly. "I don't know what though. Just looks like a map to me. Where's that to, anyways?"

Morgan shrugged. "I was just trying to think, that's all."

Askel snorted again and looked pointedly at the sand next to Morgan. He pawed his clawed feet again and shrugged out his wings.

Morgan clambered up to her feet. "I don't understand, Askel. What are you trying to say?"

Vouivre leaned over to see what all the fuss was about as well. "Oh, I see!" He snorted at Askel and the two conversed for a couple of moments. "He believes you have solved the riddle after all."

"But I haven't!" Morgan was confused. "I have no idea what the answer to the riddle is and I don't have a lot of time left to figure it out before I get eaten!" Morgan was busily working herself into a panic. "We only have a couple of hours left to figure out what it means, and I haven't the slightest clue!

"What do you think it is, Askel?" She turned to her friend and held out her arms. "The stick? The wind? The sand? What?"

Askel stepped forward again and nuzzled Morgan, trying to calm the girl down.

Vouivre stepped forward as well, crowding in close to Morgan. "As I was saying, Askel believes you may already have the answer. Obviously, you just don't realize it." He looked pointedly at the ground. "You drew a map. He believes that a map is the answer, and I happen to agree with him. It makes sense."

Morgan took a deep breath, trying to calm down. "A map?" She looked at the ground, where most of her scratching had already been kicked aside and had disappeared back into the sand. She blinked a few times as realization set in. "Rivers without water," she whispered to herself.

She reached down and picked up the stick once more. With it, she redrew the lines to represent the river. "Forests without trees." She filled in the lumpy circles with more lumps.

"Mountains without rocks." She drew in a few more mountains. "Towns without people." She remarked the area where she had marked the town. "A map."

She looked back at her friends. "A map!" She jumped forward and wrapped an arm around Askel's neck, whooping with excitement. She moved over to Vouivre and grabbed a hold of him as well, still shouting with glee. "A map!"

Tilson, Askel and Vouivre sat back and watched as Morgan began to bounce around the group, ecstatic with the knowledge that she wasn't about to be eaten. "Yes, yes, very nice," said Tilson. "Shall we go give her the answer, then?"

Morgan stopped bouncing around and came back to the group. She took a deep breath and looked at everybody. "Let's do it."

"Yeah, and the sooner she gets what she needs, the sooner we get what we need and we can get out of here." Tilson jumped up and walked towards the girl. "Seeing you all cooked from the sun, she may decide that you are ready to be eaten anyways."

The haltija took a sniff of Morgan's shirt and

grimaced. "But you go in wearing this and she's not going to want any part of that."

Morgan grinned and picked up Tilson. Even his insults couldn't dim the excitement of having the answer. With her other hand, she picked up her satchel and slung it over her shoulder once more. Looking over at the group, she asked, "Shall we?"

They headed back over to the Ancient's lair, which had filled back in with sand in their absence. To everyone's surprise, Vouivre was not able to reopen the entrance. Before he had made much progress at all, he sat back, exhausted. Morgan came over to her friend, concerned.

"Do not worry," Vouivre reassured her. "I will be all right soon. The cut from the guardian weakened me more than I had realized. Once we return to the council, I will be put back right."

That reminded Morgan. "Where is the guardian?" She looked around, half expecting to see the Ghirtablili looming behind them.

"He may still be recovering from yesterday's fight." Vouivre looked away from the partially dug hole. "Unless we don't get back with the

Ancient's answer in time, she may send him to fetch us."

Askel managed to reopen the entrance with relative ease, as the nearby workers scattered for cover again. Once the doorway was open, Tilson jumped down from his perch on Morgan's shoulder and headed over to take a seat on the gryphon's back. "We will be here when you return," the haltija waved.

Morgan shook her head and headed down the tunnel into Amahté-Baki's lair. She wasn't surprised in the slightest that Tilson had decided to stay behind.

At the door that had been too small for Vouivre to pass through, Morgan took a deep breath and steadied herself before entering. She hoped that the answer they had come up with was the correct one, but they had no better options. The waiting was the worst part, like watching a clock count down the minutes she had left. She took another steadying breath and opened the door.

As before, the room was bathed in a soft glow from the braziers that were lit at the far end of the room. Silk- and fur-covered pillows were strewn about, along with plenty of other comfortable items, such as blankets and the like. This time, however, Morgan noticed a number of other items buried among the finery.

A sword leaned up against a wall, tucked neatly between a pair of gigantic pillows. Its blade was covered in a leather sheath and its hilt was crusted with gemstones of brilliant blue. Near the sword, a shining silvery helmet rested on another pile of blankets.

Morgan shivered as she wondered if any of these items belonged to others who had come before her and failed to answer the riddle. She silently told herself to stop imagining what might happen to her if the answer was wrong. The answer had to be right. It just had to.

The Ancient sat as before, motionless at the end of the room between the braziers. When Morgan came closer, she opened her eyes and looked down at the girl. "You are early, emissary of the council. I can only hope that this means you have discovered the answer to my question."

Morgan gulped. If Askel and Vouivre were correct, she would walk out of here with the information that Stormshock needed. On the other hand, if they were wrong, she would never see any of them again. "I have." She took another deep breath.

"The answer is a map."

~ 10 ~

SHELTER

The Ancient leaned back on her haunches and smiled at Morgan. "A map. A map it is, and a map you shall receive. In the box at your side, you will find what you need. Take this back to the council; it will show you where to find the one you seek."

Morgan looked around and spotted the box fairly quickly. It was large, about the size of the boxes her parents had stored out in the garage. Although obviously made of wood, it was carved with intricate designs and inlaid with many precious stones and metals. Morgan took a couple of moments to appreciate the box before opening it.

The interior was lined with thick, soft burgundy velvet and held only one item. A scroll was tucked inside, tightly rolled and carefully tied with a deep burgundy ribbon of the same shade as the velvet.

Hesitantly, Morgan reached inside and withdrew the scroll. She gently closed the box and looked up at Amahté-Baki, who was still smiling at her.

"Thank you," she said to the Ancient. "I should get this back to the council as soon as possible."

"Yes. I am certain that your friends will be happy to see that you have survived this visit." She smiled more, a deep, knowing smile, settled back onto her haunches, and closed her eyes.

To all appearances, she was a statue once again.

Morgan wasted no time in exiting the lair. Her friends were still waiting for her outside, so she ran to them, waving the scroll. "I got a map!"

Tilson blinked at her. "You got a map?" He

stood up on Askel's back and moved forward to better see what Morgan was carrying. "You sure that's a map? It's still all tied up."

Morgan shrugged. "She said it was a map and to take it to the council." She grinned. "I'm just happy that it was the right answer after all."

As a group, they decided to waste no time in heading home to take the scroll to Stormshock. As they headed out, Morgan took one last long look at the entrance to the Ancient's lair. Even as they flew off, Morgan could see that the sand had already begun to fill in, soon looking as though the opening had never been there.

As when they arrived, Morgan and Tilson rode on Vouivre's back. This time, Askel stayed close by. Only a few hours into the flight, however, Morgan realized that they were in trouble. The wind that had made an appearance when they had discovered the answer to the riddle hadn't calmed down; in fact, it felt like it was picking up. She could feel the force of the wind, even beyond the normal amount of buffeting due to their speed. She looked around and could see trees all about them begin swaying, their branches dancing around as if to inaudible music.

Overhead, the sky changed from the light purple color that she had finally gotten accustomed to. It darkened until the sky was a deep, thick plum color as far as Morgan could see, as though the air itself was bruised. Clouds gathered low over them, darkening the sky and forming into tight knots of blackness.

Vouivre began to have trouble as the winds continued to escalate. Once they left the desert, he moved lower to seek shelter among the trees. He headed for a tight cluster of trees that appeared to be unbothered by the storm brewing overhead. "We will find shelter here until the storm has passed. I cannot take us further until then."

He landed just outside the small grove. Morgan and Tilson climbed down and followed Vouivre out of the deafening wind, with Askel following close behind. They wove among close-growing trees, which reminded Morgan of the tunnel leading to Stormshock's clearing. Soon, Vouivre led them to a small open space towards the center of the grove that was strangely devoid of wind.

A man came forward to greet them. He had tired-looking, teal eyes that glowed eerily, even in the low light that filtered in through the branches overhead. His hair was short and silver, with one braid trailing down the right side of his face. His clothing was a shirt and pair of coarse pants, both the colors of the leaves around them and the grass underfoot.

As he approached the small group, he held out both arms before him and smiled warmly. "Greetings, travelers. My name is Tellius. Why don't you come inside?" He looked up at the swaying trees far above them. "The weather seems a bit playful today."

Tellius led the group further into the grove, where another strange-looking man sat before a blazing fire. A small covered area was arranged nearby, not much more than a number of branches bent together and covered with moss.

Tellius invited the group to sit and warm themselves, for although the wind was not howling through the trees as it was doing outside, the temperature of the air in the clearing had dropped considerably.

Morgan thanked him and huddled closer to the fire, as did the rest of the group. The cooling air in the grove was nowhere as cold as the desert had been at night, but it was still cold enough that the fire was a welcome relief. Tilson moved close enough to the fire that Morgan could almost smell the burning fur but the haltija seemed comfortable.

Tellius settled in close to the fire as well, in between Morgan and the other man. Morgan noticed that the cold didn't seem to be affecting these two men as much as it did her group and she spent a moment wondering why, but decided to let it pass.

"I hope that you don't have too far of a journey ahead of you," Tellius said. "It may be a day or two before the winds let up enough for you to continue."

Morgan looked thoughtful for a moment. "I'm not sure," she replied. "I'm not even exactly sure where we are right now."

Tellius laughed. "I am not surprised. It's easy for most people to get lost in this type of weather. Right now, you are in the Biscayan Territories, just north of the Cantabrian Kingdom."

Morgan tried to think back to her geography lesson, but couldn't remember anything about Biscayan Territories or the Cantabrian Kingdom. "Where is that?"

"Spain. Northern Spain, actually. About a day's travel northwest of us is the Atlantic Ocean."

"Oh." Morgan remembered where the Atlantic Ocean was, but she couldn't remember where Spain was. She really needed to start paying more attention in her geography classes if she was going to be travelling all over the world like this.

They spent the next number of hours huddled around the fire, talking. Tellius and his companion were druids who had isolated themselves in order to be in better touch with the world around them. Tellius became quite excited when he discovered that Morgan was a chosen. He wanted to know all about the work that Morgan had been doing with the council, nodding sagely when he was told about the dragon spheres.

"I am not surprised. Dragons are one of the largest sources of fey magic right now." He chuckled at that. "Not just physically, but their magic is strong also. Unfortunately, this does explain the imbalance in the ether that we had been sensing."

"You can sense it?"

Tellius nodded. "I had hoped that there was some other explanation, but after what you have told us, there can be none. What you are doing is very important indeed. You must find a way to restore the balance and release the Ether before the veil falls completely."

"I know, Stormshock has been telling me about that, too. We think we've found a way of releasing the trapped ether." Morgan told him about the journey to meet with the Ancient and the map that should lead them to the Master Smith, who might be able to break the ether-filled orbs.

Tellius looked impressed. "You have indeed been working hard, it appears. I am sure that you will be able to find the human responsible for all of this soon."

"You are sure it's a human, too?" Morgan wasn't as sure. "Humans don't have magic and most humans don't even know about the ether."

"For the most part, I agree with you. Humans have no magic of their own but they are able to manipulate the magic of the fey as though it was theirs."

"So this is all about someone wanting power?" Morgan deflated. If it was about power, she couldn't deny the likelihood of a human being behind the attacks. She had paid enough attention in her history classes to know that humans have always wanted more power. Stormshock even said that was the reason that the veil had been put in place in the beginning, because humans were getting too greedy.

"Not necessarily," Tellius replied. "There are plenty of other reasons that someone might want to drop the veil." He leaned closer and dropped his voice to a whisper. "It may even be a former chosen."

Before Morgan could ask more about this,

there was a loud crash, as though something very heavy had fallen behind them. Morgan jumped and turned to look, and Tellius was already running over to where Vouivre had fallen.

A short distance from the fire, Vouivre lay sprawled on the ground, a far cry from the compact bundle he normally settled down into. His neck was stretched out across the grass, his head at an uncomfortable-looking angle and his eyes closed tightly. One of his massive wings had dropped onto the ground and was spread out like a wrinkled blanket; the other was still tucked under his body. His tail was curled on the ground behind him as well, as motionless as the rest of his body.

Tilson was squealing and hopping about, shouting at everyone. "Help! Oh, someone help! They've found us, and we're going to be taken next! I don't want to go!" He skittered around and hid behind Morgan. "No, no, no, no…"

Morgan scooped up the hysterical haltija and tucked him into her shirt, looking around nervously. Seeing no apparent danger, she walked closer to her motionless friend.

As she approached, she could hear the irregular, labored sound of Vouivre's breathing. "He's not dead, Tilson." She put a hand onto Vouivre's strong neck. Although Vouivre was generally a bit cool to the touch, he felt even colder than normal. She looked up at Askel. "What's wrong with him?"

Askel snorted and trotted over to the druids, who were standing side-by-side and looking over Vouivre. He snorted again and pawed at the ground. Tellius turned to look at him, listening as though he understood.

"Poison from the Ancient's guardian, hmm? I think we might be able to help with that. What type of guardian was it?"

Askel snorted a few times and bobbed his head. Tellius nodded and sent his companion off to gather supplies.

Morgan peeked in to check on Tilson. "Hear that? We aren't being attacked. It's the guardian from the Ancient's lair." Morgan winced as she said it, ashamed that she had so quickly forgotten about her friend's injury.

Tilson poked his head out and cautiously looked around. Deciding that they were no longer in danger, he climbed the rest of the way out and walked down the length of Morgan's arm to rest his small head on Vouivre's neck. "Is he gonna be okay?"

"I don't know." Morgan smoothed her hand down the length of Vouivre's neck. She could barely feel Vouivre's pulse, throbbing beneath the thick hide. "I hope so."

The men worked on Vouivre through the night, with the group of friends staying nearby. Strange poultices and foul-smelling liquids were brought over to aid in the treatments. The druids muttered among themselves, sometimes looking grimly at the gigantic fey, other times looking hopeful. As the sun crested the horizon in the morning, Vouivre finally opened an eye and looked around.

Tellius immediately moved over to speak with Vouivre, cautioning him to stay still for a while yet. "You are still weak, and need your rest. We have sent word back to the council to explain your delay. They sent back their hopes that you will make a swift recovery and are aware that you will be here for a few days yet."

He ran his hand gently over the top of

Vouivre's large head. "There is no great hurry for your return. The council is aware that the chosen is safe here and that is all that matters right now."

Vouivre slightly nodded and closed his eyes once more, settling into a more comfortable sleep. After checking him over once more and putting a gathering of herbs and flowers near Vouivre's snout, Tellius joined the rest of the group by the campfire.

"Your friend is strong indeed; most would not have survived this long after receiving this type of poison. Ghirtablili are bad news.

"Luckily, we have the necessary herbs here to fix him up, so he should be back on his feet within a day or two."

Morgan nodded, relieved that her friend would recover. None of the group had slept well that night, being so concerned over their friend. Now, knowing that he would be better soon, Morgan settled down for some rest.

When she woke, the sun was high overhead and both of the druids were over tending to Vouivre again. Tellius checked the wound on his back to see that it was healing properly and replaced the bandages covering it while the other druid, whose name she had finally learned was Lothar, fed him some sort of strange concoction. Morgan gathered herself together to check on her friend, too.

Vouivre was tired, as Morgan had expected, but he was in a surprisingly good mood as well. He smiled weakly as Morgan approached. "At least I can say that I got you out of there safely and left you in good hands while I was ill." He winced a bit in pain as the silent druid prodded a bit at the healing wound, but didn't complain.

Tellius fed Vouivre the last of the sweet-smelling paste and gathered the bowls up to leave. As he walked past Morgan, he said, "When you have a chance, I would like to speak with you." He looked up from the bowls that he was carrying to meet Morgan's eyes. "There is no hurry. I would just appreciate the chance to converse with you again."

Morgan nodded and watched the man walk away before turning back to Vouivre. "They told me that the council knows we are here, so there isn't as much of a hurry. You take your time healing and we will leave when you are ready." She smiled at her friend. "Besides, if they say you need to stay here for too long, I'm sure that Askel can give us a lift back home. That way you can have enough time to recover."

Vouivre smiled again and looked over to the druids, who were both huddled by the fire once more. "When we came down to land, I hadn't realized that they were here; I was just thinking that it would be a good place to get out of the weather for a bit. Luck must have been with us, because if they hadn't been here, Askel would likely have had to take you back to the council so that they could send someone back for me."

He watched the druids for another long moment before looking back at Morgan again. "They are good men, once chosen ones themselves. When the time came for them to rejoin the human population, however, they decided that they would rather stay as they were, not quite a part of either world, but still a part of both."

Morgan looked over to the druids as well and spent a moment thinking that it was odd that the fire never seemed to fade at all, even though she never saw anyone add more wood to it. She shrugged to herself. Perhaps they had added it while she hadn't been looking, or perhaps it was part of the magic that the fey had said humans could use. She turned back to Vouivre.

"Tellius said that you need your rest, so I'll let you sleep some more. Besides, he said that he wanted to talk to me, so I should go see what's going on."

Vouivre nodded again. "Yes, I am feeling quite tired already and I believe he has some important things to discuss with you, so you should go and speak with him." He laid his head back down on one of the rocks and closed his eyes once more.

Morgan spent a few minutes running her hand over the cool, smooth skin of Vouivre's neck before heading over to where the druids were sitting. She spent a moment warming her hands in front of the fire before turning to Tellius. "You said you wanted to speak with me?"

"Yes, I did." He excused himself from Lothar and stood up. "If you would follow me, please."

Morgan followed him over to the small shelter towards the trees and waited nearby while the druid stepped inside. Morgan would have followed but it didn't look as though there was enough room inside for two. After rummaging for only a couple minutes, Tellius stepped back outside, holding a strange necklace in his hands, which he handed to Morgan.

The necklace was large, almost the size of the green scale that Corran had given to her. It was made out of some sort of dark white material, not quite wood and not quite stone. Morgan wondered if it was bone. Rather than just a flat piece of material with a design etched into it, this one was only the design, with no background pieces.

The design was of a stylized tree, like a company would use for advertising back home. The branches were carefully spread about, with small forms carved into them. As Morgan looked closer, she spotted minuscule animals perched among the branches. The tree was attached to a braided leather cord, long enough for Morgan to loop over her neck.

"This is for you. I received it while I was a chosen, and the time has come for me to pass it along to you." Tellius smiled down at the girl. "Besides, I no longer have any use for it."

Morgan looked back up at him in surprise. "Wow. Thanks." She put the cord around her neck, being careful to not snag any of the delicate branches on her shirt. "It's really neat."

Tellius laughed. "You have no idea what that is, do you?" When Morgan shook her head, Tellius explained. "It is an Amulet of Kinship. It allows you to converse with any intelligent creature in the area, no matter what language they speak." He looked over to Askel. "So you will be able to understand what that one is saying now."

He reached out and traced a finger across a couple of branches. "It will also warn you when there is great evil being planned near you and tell you when you are being lied to."

"How will it warn me?"

"It will warm up or rattle just a bit. Not enough that others will notice but enough for you to notice."

"Wow." Morgan looked back down at the amulet, amazed. She tucked it inside her shirt, hoping that it would be safer there.

"You don't need to worry about breaking it," Tellius said, apparently guessing the reason for Morgan's actions. "It's magical. It takes a lot more effort to destroy a magical item than you'd expect." He smiled. "I wore that amulet almost every day for over ten years and not once did I even manage to scratch it. I was a clumsy child, too."

"I...I don't know how to thank you."

"No thanks are needed. I know that being a chosen can feel like a thankless job at times but I hope that this will remind you how important it is and how much we all appreciate what you're doing."

He reached back into the shelter and drew out another item. This one was a long wooden pole, almost as long as Morgan was tall. There were leather cords wrapped around it about a third of the way from the top and a small stone dangled from the end of one of the cords.

When Tellius handed the pole to Morgan, she thanked him and looked more closely at the stone. It was a dark yellow, almost orange, and roughly cut, as though it had been pulled directly out of the ground. A small hole was punched through one end for the cord to be tied through. She looked back at Tellius, hoping that there was an explanation for this as well.

"This is a Staff of Survival and it has a lot of handy tricks." He motioned for Morgan to hand the staff back to him before continuing. "First of all, this will not break either." To demonstrate, he gripped the staff by an end and swung it like a baseball bat at a nearby rock.

The staff met the stone with a resounding thud but when he showed the staff to Morgan, she could see that it wasn't even cracked.

"Also, it can help you with grabbing things that are just out of reach." He adjusted his grip on the staff and reached towards the lowest of the tree branches overhead. To Morgan's amazement, the end of the staff curled over back towards itself and Tellius was able to hook the end over the branch to pull it down. He let go of the branch and the end went back straight again.

"It has two ways to do that, too. Not just the hook for pulling, but also a claw for actual grabbing." With another adjustment to his grip on the staff, he made the same end of the pole split into three pieces, which he then used to reach down and pluck a blade of grass from the ground. "It's all in how you hold it, you see."

Morgan nodded in wonder, amazed by this marvelous staff. "How does it do all of that?"

Tellius slid his hand down the pole to the wrapped cording and showed Morgan the crystal that was attached there. "This is embedded with magic, very strong magic. It also allows the staff to be able to purify water so that it is safe to drink and lead you to shelter when you need it."

He grinned once more. "It has another enchantment on it, one that I am proud to say that I added myself." He reached out and set the staff on the ground with the end resting on the grass. With a wink to Morgan, he let go.

Morgan watched, speechless again as the staff didn't fall. It just stood there, exactly as Tellius had left it. "How does it do that?"

"Just a minor enchantment, nothing big. I got tired of setting it down in the woods and having to look around at all of the wood on the ground to figure out which one was my staff and which was a fallen branch." He reached out and took the staff again, handing it back to Morgan. "I know that you will take good care of it."

Morgan nodded and accepted the staff. "I will, I promise."

"We have one last thing for you. This one is specifically from Lothar." He reached into the shelter one last time and brought out a bundle of cloth. "This will allow you to be concealed whenever you need it. All you have to do is pull the hood over your head and hold still." He draped the cloak over Morgan's shoulders.

Morgan held out an arm and looked over the cloak, which was the same green and brown pattern as the druids wore. "You mean, when I am wearing this, people really can't see me?" She looked back at Tellius. "Or does it just make it harder for people to see me when I am in the woods?" Morgan had heard of camouflage, which was what the military wore to not be seen by the people they were fighting against.

"No matter where you are, in the forest, in the sand, or even in the snow, as long as you have the hood up and you are not moving, you would have to be stepped on to be noticed."

"So this is actual magic, too? Like the staff

and the amulet?" When Tellius nodded, Morgan looked back down at the cloak. It covered her from her shoulders all the way to the ground, the hem just barely brushing against the grass at her feet. "That's amazing."

Morgan spent the next couple of days working with Tellius to get the hang of using the new tools that she had been given. She had a lengthy conversation with a curious squirrel about the merits of different varieties of nuts and berries. She watched and listened as a flock of birds flew overhead, marveling at the discussion that she was only able to hear a brief part of, something about a good resting spot a short distance to the south.

She stayed up late at night, talking with Askel for the first time, overjoyed that she could finally understand what the gryphon was saying to her. Tellius showed her how to use the staff to make fresh water and find shelter and soon Morgan was wandering all over the camp, picking up everything in sight with the clawed end. She snuck up on Tilson more than once with her cloak, delighting in making the haltija jump in surprise.

During all of this, Vouivre steadily improved. He got stronger and was able to stay awake throughout the third day. By sundown on the fourth day, Tellius and Lothar proclaimed him ready to make the journey home.

Morgan, Vouivre, Tilson and Askel each thanked the druids for their hospitality and their aid before packing up all of their belongings and taking to the sky once more. As they flew off, Morgan looked back one last time at the druids' grove, hoping that she would meet them again someday.

~ 11 ~

MAGICGLEAM

Corran was surprised to see the group as they landed in the clearing on Zea Island. He came forward to greet them and held out his hands in welcome. "We were not expecting you for another day or so, but we are all pleased at your safe return.

"I am informed that you have met with success."

Morgan dropped from Vouivre's back and grinned at the elvor. "We did, and Amahté-Baki gave us this." She pulled the scroll from her pack and held it up before her so that Corran could see it. "She said it's a map so that we can find the Master Smith that Stormshock has been looking for."

Corran nodded and examined the scroll. "I trust you didn't have too much trouble." Looking up at Vouivre, he quickly amended, "Besides the problem with the guardian, I mean. We knew that there would be a guardian there; we just weren't expecting one as powerful as the Ghirtablili."

"She gave me a riddle to solve." Morgan dug into her pack and pulled out the book that she had written the riddle in and read it to Corran.

The elvor looked puzzled. "A riddle? I thought that was just a myth."

Morgan grinned. "I thought you guys were all just myths."

"You do have a point." Corran smiled. He indicated the scroll that Morgan had dropped back into her satchel. "You should bring that to Stormshock. I know that he has been eagerly waiting for your return."

Morgan nodded and put the book away. Pulling the strap of the satchel more securely onto her shoulder, she headed towards the path that led to the dragon's pool.

Once she was in the clearing, she fairly ran down the path to the rocks that she normally perched on top of. She started calling to her friend as she climbed, a little surprised that he hadn't reacted to her arrival as he usually did.

"Stormshock, we're back. We got a map to find the..." She trailed off in mid-sentence and stared at the pool in horror.

Floating in the center was a swirling green sphere.

Time slowed to a crawl, yet seemed to fly past at the same time. Morgan didn't remember how she got out of Stormshock's clearing. She didn't remember how she got the orb out of the water. She didn't remember climbing back down off the rocks surrounding the pool. She didn't remember walking back down the path and back out to where the rest of the council waited. All she knew was that Corran was there, holding her upright because her knees wouldn't hold her up anymore. He was trying to find out why she was wet and Morgan had no idea what to say.

Soundlessly, Morgan held out her hand and showed Corran the orb.

Corran took it and, more gently than Morgan would have expected, lowered her to the ground. He waved one of the other fey to come and watch over Morgan before quickly striding down the tunnel towards the pool. Morgan watched as the elvor disappeared from sight.

Askel came over to Morgan and nuzzled her with his beak. Morgan wrapped her arms around the gryphon and buried her face in the soft feathers of his neck.

Some time later, Morgan had no idea of how much, Corran came back out of the tunnel and looked grimly at the rest of the gathered fey. He walked over to Askel, who was still trying to comfort Morgan. "I know that you want to stay with your friend but this needs to be delivered as well. I trust that you will take good care of it." He held up a leather pouch with a strap that was long enough to go around the gryphon's neck.

Askel dropped his head towards Corran, allowing the fey to loop the pouch over his head.

"What's going on? Where's Askel going?" Morgan tried to shake off some of the numb feeling that had spread throughout her body and coated her brain, making it hard to understand anything. She looked over at Askel. "Where are you going?"

Corran spoke up and answered for the gryphon. "Before you set out to meet with the Ancient, Stormshock found a caretaker for the spheres and a few young hatchlings that had been discovered. With Stormshock now gone, Askel will be taking this to Magicgleam as well, and she will be guarding them until we are able to release the ether."

"Can I come, too?" Morgan looked at Corran pleadingly.

Corran seemed to think about this. "I am not sure that would be wise. Magicgleam takes her position as guardian quite seriously."

"Can't we just tell her that I have been the one finding the spheres? I mean, I am the one that's been doing all this to save you guys and all." Although she knew that Stormshock was gone and there wasn't anything she could do to bring him back, Morgan wasn't ready to let go of him. Not quite yet. All of a sudden, it had become very important to her to make sure that this last piece of him was safe.

"Please?"

Corran looked towards the group of shocked fey that had gathered in the clearing at the news of Stormshock's disappearance. None of them seemed to have any objections to sending her, so Corran looked back to Morgan. "Be very careful. I don't want to have to find another chosen already."

Morgan let out a whoop of triumph and climbed onto Askel's back. Before they could leave, however, Corran stopped them. "Wait!"

Morgan settled herself comfortably onto Askel's back and caught Tilson, who had apparently decided to come along as well. If Corran had changed his mind about letting her go, he was not going to have an easy time getting her off of the gryphon. "What?"

"The scroll, give it to me. While you are gone, I can at least try to figure out where you are supposed to go next."

"Oh, right." Morgan rummaged through her pack, surprised to see that the contents were dry. After having been in Stormshock's pool, she had expected everything to be soaked. "Nothing's wet!" She looked back over at Corran.

"Of course nothing's wet; it's not supposed to be. That satchel will keep anything in it safe and dry, and it will be able to hold pretty much anything you need to have." He held out his slender hand. "The scroll, if you please."

Morgan pulled it out and handed it over. "Amahté-Baki said it was a map, so it shouldn't be too hard to find where we need to go."

Corran nodded and took the scroll. "Some maps are easier to read than others so I want to be sure of where you are going before I send you off on a wild chase." He tucked the scroll into his shirt.

"Now be off, and send my thanks again to Magicgleam."

As Askel started to run towards the edge of the clearing, Morgan leaned forward and buried her face again in the gryphon's feathers, taking care to leave Tilson enough room to breathe between them. As they leapt into the air and flew off, Morgan tried to blame her watery eyes on the wind.

Morgan dozed on the journey, drifting in and out of sleep. She woke up completely when they landed in a large grassy field. "Where are we?"

"Halkirk Island," Askel responded. "Magicgleam's lair is not too far from here."

Morgan dropped to the ground and caught Tilson, settling the haltija into the hood of her sweatshirt. She looked around, not seeing much but a large meadow and a few scattered boulders off to the south. "Where?"

Askel walked towards the pile of boulders. "This is not a place that is known by humans. Magicgleam's lair is beyond those stones."

Morgan and Tilson followed close behind Askel. Just to be safe, Morgan pulled Stormshock's scale from the pack and held it in her hand. Corran had told her that the scale would notify the fey that she was sent by Stormshock, so Morgan hoped that it would still work with this guardian. She wondered if this guardian would attack them like the Ghirtablili had, or help them as Kun and Einar had.

She rubbed her thumb along the ridges where the symbol was etched into the scale. While she was holding the scale like that, she realized that no matter what happened from this point on, she had a piece of her friend to keep with her. The thought soothed her somewhat, and she clutched the precious scale close to her chest.

As the small group approached the rocks, Morgan realized that the boulders were a lot larger than she had first thought, mostly because they were not standing upright but were lying on the ground. If they had been standing, Morgan guessed that each of the stones would be more than ten feet tall.

In the center of the ring of stones, Askel stopped and motioned for the rest of them to gather close in to him. Once they were all close enough to touch, he spread his wings to wrap around them. Pulling them in tightly against his body, he reached out with one of his claws and began to scratch at the ground.

The size of Askel's wings kept Morgan from being able to see what he was scratching, and the strength of those wings kept her from pulling away far enough to see. Morgan gave up trying to watch and settled against Askel's warm flank.

Slowly, almost too slowly for Morgan to realize what was happening, the world started to spin. Not just at the super-slow creeping pace that Morgan knew that the world always spun in, but in a really fast way. It felt like when she would sit in her father's office chair and turn herself around and around until she could no longer stand up straight. She clung to Askel to keep from falling over. Her stomach heaved with the motion and she hoped she wasn't going to get sick.

Eventually the dizziness subsided and Askel let go of Morgan and Tilson. Morgan held still for a moment to let the queasiness subside before she looked around, blinking in surprise. Although she could tell that they were in the same place as they had started, the stones that had been lying around them were now standing up. They were not ten feet tall, as Morgan had initially thought. Instead, they were more like twelve to fifteen feet high. These pillars formed the entrance to a walkway made of light grey stones that led off into the distance.

Askel led them along the walkway, cautioning them not to step off the stone walk. "If you touch the grass, you will be back out in the meadow once more." Morgan wasn't sure how necessary his words of warning were since the stone path was at least five feet across. Nevertheless, she made sure to stay as close to the center as she could.

The path led down to a large platform, almost as wide across as Stormshock's pool had been. In the center of this platform was a flight of steps, also made of stone, heading down underground.

Morgan and Tilson followed Askel down the stairs and she wondered at the sheer number of steps and how far down they had gone before hitting the bottom. It felt as though they had walked down the distance of the Grand Canyon.

On the way down, Morgan had a chance to think back and realize just how much of her time was spent underground since becoming involved with the fey. Although this disturbed her a little bit, she realized that the rest of the time with the fey was more than worth it.

At the base of the steps, they found themselves in a chamber. It was large, but nowhere near as large as the room under the pyramid that they had made camp in while in the desert.

A voice met them as they stepped into the room.

"Greetings to you once again, Askel. I see you have brought me visitors." At the far end of the room, the stone wall moved and Morgan realized that the wall was not made of stone at all, nor was it even a wall. A gigantic dragon was sitting a short distance from them, with scales of such a pure silver color that they reflected the stone walls on either side. Its wings were close in to its body and the creases where they were folded looked just like the seams in the stone walls, further adding to the disguise. Its taloned feet were splayed on the ground, a much less brilliant silver color so that they looked like sharpened rocks against the cavern floor. When the dragon opened her eyes, Morgan noticed that they were also bright, reflective silver colored, tinged slightly with blue.

Askel bowed to the dragon as she revealed herself. Seeing this, Morgan decided that it couldn't hurt to be polite and bowed as well.

"Ahh, and you have not brought me just any visitor now, have you? Unless I am mistaken, this is the council's newest chosen." Morgan looked up in surprise at this recognition of her, so the dragon smiled and continued. "And I see you have brought Stormshock's mark with you to prove it."

Morgan looked down at the green scale, still clenched in her hand. Unsure how to respond, she remained silent.

"To what do I owe this visit?" she looked towards Askel once more.

Askel stepped forward and bowed again, this time dipping his head so that the pouch slid off his neck and dropped gently to the floor. With one taloned claw, he opened the pouch and withdrew the shining green sphere.

Magicgleam fell silent. Slowly, she reached out with one massive claw to pick up the orb. "Is this what it looks like?" She looked between Morgan and Askel, as if she was not sure which one would respond.

Morgan answered first. "I found it this morning." She didn't meet the dragon's eyes but kept her gaze firmly on the toes of her shoes. "It was floating in his pool." Although her throat constricted at the words and she still felt like crying at the loss of her friend, Morgan knew that Stormshock would want her to be strong.

"I see." Morgan looked up to see her turning the sphere around in her claw and looking deeply into it. Catching Morgan's gaze, the dragon turned to face her. "And what of you, child? I know that you have been sent to find the source. Have you discovered who is behind all of this?" She loomed over her, almost threatening in her intensity.

Morgan stuttered and had to clear her throat before answering. "Not quite yet. Everyone seems to be sure that it's a human behind it, but nobody seems to know who. There are rumors that it may be a former chosen but we just don't know yet."

Magicgleam exhaled, sending a stream of hot steam down over them. "What of your meeting with the Ancient one? I see you survived the encounter."

"Y...Yes. We were able to come up with an answer to her riddle and she gave us a scroll. She said it was a map."

"And where does this map lead to?" She

leaned down even closer to Morgan, her silver eyes flashing.

"I don't... I don't know. Corran has it, back at Zea Island. I haven't seen what's inside it." Morgan took a breath. "He's looking over it, trying to find out where to send us next." She was having a hard time focusing on the dragon; her reflective nature made it amazingly difficult to keep her mind and her eyes steady. Trying to make her head a bit less cluttered, she blinked her eyes five or six times in rapid succession.

Magicgleam nodded slightly and backed up, putting a much more comfortable amount of distance between her and Morgan. "Very well. I will keep this safe," she said as she held up the sphere, "while you find a way to release the magic." She backed up further and closed her claw around the orb. Closing her eyes, she faded back into the stones, blending into her surroundings until Morgan could no longer see her at all.

Askel led them back out of the chamber and up the stairs, where they all paused to take a number of deep, clearing breaths. Tilson sat straight onto the stones outside the stairway, rubbing at his face, especially his eyes. Morgan, with her hands on her knees and bent almost double, looked over at Askel. "Is she always intimidating like that?"

Askel nodded.

They didn't have to walk all the way back up to the entrance of the stone path. Just as Askel had warned them on the way in, as soon as they jumped down to the grass, the stone disappeared. There was a brief moment of disorientation, nowhere near as bad as it had been on the way in, and they were back out in the grass once more.

Askel flew them directly back to Zea Island, since they were all eager to find out what Corran had discovered in their absence. The sun was just starting to set as they arrived, so not many fey remained in attendance. Corran was still there and they headed directly towards the elvor.

"Did you find anything?" Morgan asked.

"Yes and no," Corran answered. "The scroll is a map as you said it would be, but I am not certain of the wisdom in sending you to the place it shows."

"Why not?"

"It is a very dangerous place for a human to enter." When Morgan just blinked at him, Corran explained. "The map shows the location of Volcan. I have looked into this and what I have found gives me great pause." As if to accentuate that, he took a couple seconds to make eye contact with each of them.

"Volcan is a smith of great talent who is rumored to be able to make anything. He has a great hammer of tremendous power that allows him to craft anything that he wishes. This is the item that we need to break the spheres and release the magic back into the ether.

"The problem, however, is twofold. First, Volcan is highly possessive of his hammer, and is not likely to let anyone, not even a chosen, walk away with it. This means that you will have to obtain the hammer by other means.

"The second part of the problem is the location where the map says Volcan can be found. There is a small island chain in the middle of the ocean, far to the west of us. One of these islands is nothing more than an active volcano. It is inside there that Volcan lives. From what I have been able to gather, the activity of the island is from Volcan as he works at his forge."

Corran looked back at Morgan. "That is why I don't want to send you there. It is far too dangerous for a human."

Morgan blinked at the elvor. "This guy lives inside a volcano? I mean, a really *real* volcano, not like Cinderflare's lair was?"

Corran shook it head. "As I understand, it is an enormous forge inside of a standard volcano, so it has elements of both, making it that much more dangerous. I will see what I can find to allow you safe passage into Volcan's lair. Until then, Askel will return you to your home."

~ 12 ~

VOLCANO

Liore had been busy in Morgan's absence. When she got home, she discovered that she had barely passed her math test, written a report for her science class, beaten her high score on Call of Duty, and gotten her grounded from her gaming console for a week for not doing the dishes or taking out the trash.

Morgan spent the entire first day home sitting at the window in her room, staring out at the horizon and hoping to see either Askel or Vouivre coming out to get her. The second day, she cleaned up the mess that Liore had made of her room and packed a change of clothing into her satchel, wanting to be prepared in case she was sent out for a long time again. By the third day, she had started to settle back down into her normal at-home routine. She still looked out the windows as she walked past, hoping to see her friends, but none of them appeared. Even Tilson had been conspicuously absent.

She started sketch after sketch of Tilson, Askel, and even tried to draw Corran, but her thoughts were on Stormshock most of the time. A few times she started a drawing of him, only to find herself wiping tears away almost as soon as she started to draw.

A couple of times, her mother peeked in on her while she was in her room and Morgan quickly covered the sketches with homework papers that Liore had conveniently left behind. Morgan could tell that her mother knew something was bothering her because there was a little wrinkle between her eyebrows whenever she was faced with something she didn't have an answer to. There were a couple of times when it appeared as though she was going to come in and try to talk with Morgan, but her phone would ring and she would turn back to her business, leaving Morgan alone with her thoughts.

One evening, her mother came into Morgan's room and sat on her bed. "How is school going?"

Morgan shrugged. "About usual, I guess. I think I need more paper, though."

"Did something happen there that upset you?"

Morgan shook her head. She couldn't tell her about all of the things that were going on, so she decided to go with a more acceptable explanation. "I just miss all my friends, that's all."

Her mother nodded. "I know that leaving them behind was hard but I had thought you would make new ones here, too."

Morgan sighed. She hated lying to her mother, but there was no way she could get around it. "I'm still getting used to things here. Maybe later I will start to make new friends."

"What about boys? I remember there were a couple you liked in your last school, any of them here?"

"Not really. Most of 'em are too into their

own stuff to really bother with yet and the rest already have girlfriends."

That wasn't entirely untrue. The times that she had been in school, when Liore hadn't been substituting for her, there had been a couple of boys in her class that she had been looking at but she didn't really feel like she had anything in common with them. When she had first moved to this town, she had felt like an outsider and the time she spent with the fey only enhanced her sense of distance from the rest of the kids in her school.

While she was in school the next day, Morgan stopped by the library and checked out an atlas, determined that the next time she was sent out she would at least know where she was going. Maybe, she thought, she would even be able find out where she had been. She flipped to the page that showed the whole world and tried to find Egypt, curious to know how far they had flown. It took her almost ten minutes to find it and even then, she was surprised. Until she saw it on the map, she had thought Egypt was in Europe somewhere.

"At least I was close," she thought to herself. "It's almost in Europe."

A week passed without any word from Tilson, Askel, or any of the fey. Morgan finished out the remainder of the grounded time that Liore had earned for her in her room, drawing some of the amazing fey she had met and checking and rechecking her satchel to be sure that she would be ready to go when they sent for her. Soon, she started to wonder if they were ever going to send for her at all. Maybe Corran had decided that it was too risky after all and had sent someone else in her place. Maybe she had been replaced as the chosen completely. Morgan didn't like the idea of not knowing what happened to her friends, not knowing whether they were in trouble and needed her.

The more Morgan thought about it, the more convinced she was that her friends were in danger. She suspected that the council had sent them out to the volcano to retrieve Volcan's hammer without her and they couldn't do it on their own. That was the point of having a human with them: there were things that humans could do that fey couldn't. Morgan went to her closet and pulled out her satchel. She was going to go rescue her friends. They needed her.

She turned and headed for the window, stumbling over something small halfway across the room.

"Why you big-footed, little-brained, bubble-butted needle noggin! Can't you look where you're going for once? You're only ten times bigger than me." Tilson sputtered as he picked himself up and glared at Morgan. "What, you don't see us for a few days and all of a sudden you can't see us at all anymore?"

His rant was cut short as Morgan reached down to scoop him up. "Tilson! Where have you been? I was starting to think you'd forgotten about me or something."

"Forgotten? Not bloody likely. How could we forget about a big clumsy oaf like you? We've been busy while you have been sitting here doing nothing, you big lazybones." The haltija looked over at Morgan and nodded.

"Well, at least you're ready to go this time. I get tired of having to drag you out of bed all the time."

Morgan put Tilson into the hood of her

sweatshirt and headed out the window. Across the lawn, she could see Askel, standing in his customary spot just inside the trees. Morgan ran across the grass to greet him. "I missed you."

The gryphon nuzzled her shoulder. "I missed you, too."

She climbed up and got settled onto the gryphon's back, putting Tilson in front of her so that he could be comfortable too.

The group flew directly to the council's island in the middle of the river. Morgan was amused to see a lot of human boats out on the water, all of them unconsciously avoiding the land mass that she knew none of them realized was there. She looked out at all of the humans playing in the water and waved, knowing full well that none of them would wave back. She smiled and stretched out her arms to both sides, reveling in the feeling of the wind against her skin and Askel's beating wings beneath her. She smiled up into the bright sky, drinking in the wonderful sunshine.

They landed in the clearing and Corran came

over to greet them. "I trust you have enjoyed your period of rest?"

Morgan slid off of Askel's back and reached back up for Tilson. "It was OK, I guess. Liore got me in a bit of trouble while I was gone but nothing too bad." She put the haltija into her hood and slid the strap of her pack over her shoulder. "Did you figure out how I'm going to get the hammer?"

Corran nodded and led her over to a small wooden table that had been set up under one of the trees. On it, Morgan could see the parchment that she had received from the Ancient, untied and unrolled. The red ribbon that had held it closed was lying alongside it on the table. Small, smooth stones at each corner kept the edges of the map to from curling closed again.

The map was a lot more intricate than Morgan had expected it to be. The edges of the paper were colored different shades of blue, with a small boat drawn along the top in fine detail. A number of islands were drawn onto the map in rich browns and greens, with some tan-colored spots as well. Trees, small patches of forest, were carefully illustrated on a couple of the islands. Rivers crisscrossed each of the land masses in a brilliant blue-green. A couple of small cities were marked as well, but what drew Morgan's attention was the large island at the bottom of the paper. In the center of the mass stood a tall mountain with a red lake on the top and puffs of grayish-white clouds around it.

As she looked closer, the clouds drifted away from the mountain and across the sea nearby. Of course the map is magical, she thought to herself. Why wouldn't it be? Almost everything that had to do with the fey involved magic, so she wasn't sure why she had assumed that the map was just a mundane scroll.

"As you may have guessed," Corran interrupted her thoughts, "this is the home of Volcan. As I mentioned before, it is an active volcano, with eruptions every couple of days or so for the last millennia." He pointed to a small, rocky outcropping along the eastern edge of the mountain. "This is the entrance. It is the only way that my scouts have found that will lead inside." He pointed to a fairly level section of rock a little further down the mountain from the entrance. "Askel will drop you here. There is no way for him to follow you inside. Tilson, however, will be joining you."

Tilson sputtered and squeaked and started to rant, but Corran overrode him. "You said you wanted to help her in this. You cannot do that from outside."

Corran looked back up at Morgan as he continued. "Of course, Liore has already been sent to stand in your place in your absence."

"There is another item that we have prepared for you. This should be enough to allow you to undertake this task." He signaled off into the trees and another fey approached, carrying a small box.

Morgan recognized this fey from the first time she had been to the island to meet with the council. He was part man, part horse, and completely bald but for a small patch of hair on his chin that made Morgan think of a goat. She remembered thinking that the man was riding on the back of a horse the first time she had come to the island, which made her realize how much her perceptions had changed in the short period of time that had passed since then. The fey placed the box onto the table and nodded to Morgan and Corran before backing a couple steps away.

"Thank you, Arien. That will be all." Corran bowed to the fey before turning back to Morgan. He opened the box and pulled out a small clear jar that was filled with a dark yellow substance.

When Corran held it up to the light, Morgan could see that it was thick enough to barely let any light through at all. She reached out to take the jar and looked at it more closely. "What is it?"

"It is a salve. Before you enter Volcan's lair, both you and Tilson need to spread some of this onto your skin. Be careful to apply it everywhere, because this salve will be the only thing keeping the two of you from being cooked alive."

Morgan nodded and held the jar with a bit more care.

"You have a timepiece, yes?" Morgan nodded, looking down at the watch that her father had bought for her last Christmas. "This salve will only work for five hours. After that, it will start to wear off as you sweat under it. You must be on your way out by then, if not already on your way back here."

Morgan nodded again. She didn't think that she would need more than five hours to find a hammer. "This hammer... how will I know which one it is? You said he was a Master Smith, so wouldn't that mean he has lots of them?"

Now it was Corran's turn to nod. "Yes, he has many of them, and not just any hammer will do." The elvor looked up and surveyed the fey that were milling around in the clearing. "Meliai, please approach."

A fey that Morgan hadn't met walked slowly towards the table. She had long hair, reaching almost to her knees. It was loose, flowing, and a rich brown tinged with green. Her skin was a much lighter brown and very rough. To Morgan, it looked as though she was covered in the bark of a tree. She slowly stepped across the grass and silently looked between Corran and Morgan.

Corran smiled at the fey and looked over to Morgan. "This is Meliai, one of the forest guardians. She generally prefers to not interact with humans but she is willing to make an exception in this case. Meliai is one of the few fey that has actual knowledge of what Volcan's hammer looks like." He gave Morgan a moment before asking, "Do you have your notebook with you?"

Morgan nodded and slipped her pack off her shoulder. Reaching inside, she dug through the assorted stuff that she'd crammed into it and retrieved the notebook and a pencil. These she offered over to Corran.

Corran smiled and thanked her before opening the notebook. He looked for a moment at the riddle of the Ancient before turning to a fresh sheet. "One of these days, I will have to ask you the answer to this riddle. With all of the events as of late, I haven't had much time to ponder it." When Morgan started to respond, Corran stopped her. "Do not tell me yet; I am looking forward to the time when I will be able to think upon it and try to deduce the answer myself. For you to tell me now would remove the amusement."

Morgan closed her mouth and watched as Corran slid the notebook and pencil over in front of Meliai. The fey spoke in soft, musical tones for a moment, and finally the rough-skinned girl picked up the pencil. She looked the length of the pencil for a couple moments, from the tip that was already in need of another sharpening, through the tooth marks that Morgan had left along the length as she chewed on the pencil while trying to come up with an answer for the Ancient, and to the end of the pencil where the eraser was dirty and worn. She pursed her lips, and a slight frown of disapproval creased her forehead.

Corran spoke with her more and Morgan had the distinct impression that she was not pleased but soon she scowled, pressed the pencil to the paper, and began to draw.

Meliai sketched for over an hour but Morgan never got tired of watching her. She grumbled and scowled, baring her teeth at the paper any time she made a mistake in the drawing. She tried the eraser once but quickly decided that her finger worked better for smudging out unwanted pencil marks. When the tip got too worn down to draw cleanly, she put the tip of the pencil in her mouth and bit off part of the wood to sharpen it. Finally, she slammed the book closed, dropped the pencil on top of it, and stalked away.

Corran sighed and picked up the book, opening it and taking a look at the drawing she had made. He nodded slightly before handing both the book and the pencil over to Morgan.

"First of all, I hope that you take no offense to her actions. Meliai dislikes humans on principle and she has had almost no interaction with any of you."

"As for the drawing, she says that this is what the hammer looked like the last time it was used and it is extremely rare for a smith to change a completed weapon. Find the hammer that looks like this and bring it back.

"Just remember: you have only five hours of survival once you enter the lair, so be swift about it."

Morgan tucked the book and pencil into her pack. Realizing that Corran was not going to add any more, she headed over to Askel, scooping up the still-protesting haltija on the way. Although she had concerns of her own about the idea of heading into an active volcano, she had enough faith in her friends to believe that they wouldn't send her into the lair if they didn't believe that she would be able to get back out in time.

Silently, Morgan and Tilson climbed onto Askel's back and settled down. Morgan wasn't sure how long this flight would take so she decided to just sit back and enjoy the ride, hoping that it wouldn't be the last she had with her friends.

They flew for a full day, over ocean, land, oceans and more land. Morgan held on tight as they flew over tall, snow-peaked mountains and watched in awe as they flew over a school of dolphins playing in the waves. Human settlements twinkled with millions of colored lights everywhere, both over land and on boats in the water.

Finally, they landed on another island in the middle of a beautiful green sea. As Morgan dismounted, she realized that it was less of an island and more of an enormous mountain that started deep below in the water and crested high above the clouds. Although she had flown over many mountains on Askel's back, she didn't remember having seen any that were this colossal.

Tilson dropped onto the mountainside next to her, pulling his tiny pack down with him. He looked off to the south, where plumes of steam rose off the mountain, from as high as they could see and all the way down to the water, where the size of the steam clouds more than doubled in size. He took a couple steps backwards towards the gryphon and attempted to climb back up onto Askel's back.

Morgan took hold of the haltija and tucked him into the hood of her sweater. As he calmed down, she looked up the side of the mountain and was barely able to see the outcropping of rock that Corran had shown them on the map. Somehow, she had thought that Askel would be dropping them a lot closer to the opening than he had. "It's going to take us all day to climb that!"

"I am sorry," Askel apologized. "This was the closest that I could get and still be able to land securely."

"I know," Morgan grumbled. She turned and

hugged the gryphon tightly. "You'll still be here when we come back out, right?"

Askel stretched out a front claw and tucked it gingerly around the girl. "Of course I will be here, no matter how long it takes you. I have no intention of going anywhere."

Morgan buried her face in the soft feathers of Askel's neck. "We won't be long. Once we get inside, we have five hours. We'll be out way before that."

She backed away from her friend and reached into her satchel. From it, she pulled the jar of dark yellow salve that Corran had given her. She unscrewed the cap and sniffed, wrinkling her nose. "This stuff smells awful!"

"Maybe so, but remember to cover everywhere."

She tucked the jar back into her pack, not wanting to use it now and waste valuable time on the climb up the mountain. Once they were completely ready, she and the haltija picked up their packs and Morgan's staff and headed up the side of the volcano.

The climb was slow going but much easier than Morgan had expected. As far as they had to climb, she was just glad that the side they were going up was not too steep. There were plenty of handholds to help them in their ascent, as well as a number of rocks that jutted out of the ground in front of them. By nightfall, they arrived at the outcropping at the entrance to Volcan's mountain.

She placed the jar of salve on a small, flat rock nearby and scooped out some of the viscous goo. Taking a deep breath, she smeared it onto her arms and started to rub it in. "Tilson, come back out. You need this, too."

Tilson climbed down as well and began to coat himself in the substance, taking care to work it into his fur and against his skin.

It took the better part of an hour for the two of them to coat themselves, discovering that it didn't smell nearly as badly once it had been worked into the skin. Morgan double-checked that she and Tilson had covered themselves fully before recapping the jar and putting it back into her satchel.

The pair started moving into the cavern before darkness had fully settled. They had already used up a portion of the time that the salve was supposed to work and neither of them wanted to push their luck any further than necessary.

Inside the cave, Morgan was surprised. She had been in a number of mountainside lairs already and this was pretty much the same as most of them had been. Somehow, she had expected it to be much different.

The pair of them crept slowly and carefully into the maze of tunnels that lay inside the entrance, quickly finding that most of them circled back to the opening once again. After a number of these false starts, they finally found a tunnel that wound deeper inside.

As they got further into the mountain, Morgan turned on her flashlight and played it over the smooth surface of the tunnel around them. She suspected that this particular tunnel had once had lava flowing from it because the walls and floor looked burnt, as though something very hot had melted all of the rock around them. Deeper and deeper they walked in silence until finally Tilson spoke.

"I think I hear something up there." He

crawled down from his perch on Morgan's shoulder and scampered ahead to have a look.

Morgan followed not too far behind, soon realizing that the light was becoming less necessary as they went. From ahead, a dim reddish light had started to glow in the darkness. Once the light became bright enough to navigate by, she switched off the flashlight and tucked it back into her pack.

Closer they crept until finally the tunnel opened into another large cavern. Carefully, the pair peeked into the large, brightly-lit room, covering their eyes from the glare.

The cavern was a mess. Tables appeared to be randomly placed throughout the room with various tools and other implements that Morgan couldn't identify piled on them. Barrels of strange-smelling powders, foul-smelling liquids, and metal shavings were all over. Many more barrels were overflowing with debris. Fires burned everywhere Morgan looked, many with pots and other cooking and melting implements hanging in them, a few with long pieces of metal sticking out of them.

The sound of hammering echoed through

the chamber, as though someone was pounding two pieces of metal together. As Morgan looked around, she realized that there were a lot of hammers here, and she would need a better look to find the one she had been sent for.

With another careful look around the room, she snuck over to the closest barrel and peeked around it. Still seeing no one, she crept further into the room, with Tilson not far behind. They moved around the walls, slowly moving closer to the center of the chamber. Soon, the pounding stopped, and Morgan quickly slid under the closest table to hide.

She sat there in silence for a few minutes before daring to move. She poked her head out from under the table and scanned the area. What she saw amazed her.

Not fifteen feet before her, on one of the tables that she had already passed sat a hammer that she hadn't noticed only moments before. Quietly, she pulled out the sketch that Meliai had drawn of the hammer and held it up.

It was the hammer she needed.

With a cursory glance around the room once

more, she darted out into the open and grabbed the hammer.

As soon as she laid a hand on it, however, she was yanked backwards off her feet and found herself flying across the room, in the wrong direction and without the hammer she had come for. She hit the wall with a bone-jarring thud and slid to the ground, pain exploding everywhere and her vision began to fade as she saw a pair of men moving in unison.

After a moment, she realized that there wasn't a pair of them after all; it just appeared that way because of how hard her head had hit the wall. One man, taller than even Kun had been, with long, tangled hair and a beard that was tucked into his belt was walking towards her, and she tried to budge but her arms and legs refused to respond. All she could do was whimper as he grabbed her again.

"Apparently you were right after all. Let me get rid of this, and we can talk."

The last thing that Morgan thought as she lost consciousness was that he wasn't talking to her.

~ 13 ~

TRAPPED

Morgan's head was throbbing. She groaned and reached a hand up to the back of her head, feeling the swollen lump crusted with blood that the wall had left behind. She opened an eye, which did absolutely no good. Wherever she was, it was darker than anything she had seen before. When she moved her head to look around, the motion sent a wave of dizziness like she had never felt before flowing through her.

Stifling a moment of panic, she reached out a hand, almost afraid of what she might feel. To her surprise, she felt only wall. It was a smooth wall, much like the ones leading into Volcan's workshop. She groaned again and crawled across the floor, praying that her pack had survived, especially her flashlight. When she bumped into something small and furry, she couldn't keep the yelp of surprise and fear from escaping.

Her scream was joined by another, smaller wail. When she quieted, she recognized the second voice as belonging to Tilson, and reached out for him again.

"No, no, please, don't eat me! I don't taste good, I swear!" The panicked haltija babbled as Morgan scooped him up.

"Shh, it's me. Calm down." She smoothed his fur as he quieted. "Better?"

Tilson whimpered, but Morgan could feel him nod as she petted him. "Where are we?"

"I have no idea." She put the frightened haltija into her hood and went back to looking for her pack. "I need my flashlight, or we're never going to find our way back out of here." Finally, her fingers found the rough material of her satchel and she let out a sigh of relief as she pulled out the light and clicked it on.

They were in a small chamber made of the

same smooth rock as the rest of the lair had been. There was only one tunnel leading out of the room they had been dropped in and there wasn't even a door to block them from leaving. Somehow, Morgan knew that this couldn't end well. She slung her pack over her shoulder and considered their options. "I guess we have to try it, hmm?"

She walked towards the exit but only got about halfway there before she could feel a rumbling under her feet. "That can't be good." She raced towards the tunnel and kept on running. There weren't any exits leading off the tunnel that they were on but that didn't relieve any of Morgan's apprehension. Forward she ran, hoping against hope that they would make it out of here soon. All of that came to a stop when she rounded a corner and the wall opened up into a pool of lava.

The lava she could have handled, she thought, if it weren't for the strange creature that seemed to be *swimming* in the pool. She skittered to a stop as the beast turned towards them.

It had a slinky, serpentine body covered with

copper and red scales. Worse than that, it had more than one head. Seven long necks protruded from the creature's body, each with a head the size of a small car. Three of the heads moved over in front of Morgan and Tilson, blocking off their path. One of the heads opened its maw, filled with rows of wickedly curved fangs, and exhaled a plume of flame at them.

Morgan shrieked and dove back into the tunnel that they had been in, barely avoiding the geyser of fire as it blew over them. She rolled back and out of the way, not stopping until she could no longer see any of the lava. "I think we have to find another way out."

Tilson shook himself off; he had fallen out of her hood as she rolled. "Actually, I think we need to get past it to get out."

Morgan blinked at him. "You can't be serious."

The haltija nodded. "There's a gate up at the other end of the path, on the other side of the lava. It's probably there to keep that thing down here." He finished brushing the dirt from his fur and stood up to face her. "And now us, too."

Morgan looked at him for a long moment before creeping forward to peek around the corner once more. The enormous beast was no longer paying attention to them and she could see that Tilson had been correct. Not only did the path go up on the other side of the lake but there was a barred exit almost directly across from them. She sat back on the ground and leaned against the wall of the tunnel.

"So how do we get past it?"

"I have no idea." He walked over to her and climbed up into her hood again.

Morgan considered their options. She knew that because of the salve they could survive the heat and fire that was all around them in the volcano but she doubted that protection would include swimming across a lake of lava. Not to mention the creature that was waiting out there to incinerate and probably eat them as soon as they stepped out of their tunnel.

Suddenly, she remembered something, and it just might work. "I have an idea."

"Nope," Tilson answered. "I am not bait and I am not going to lure it away so you can get out." He crossed his arms and settled deeper into her hood. "Not gonna happen."

"No, I wasn't thinking that." She pulled her pack off and began digging through it. "I know I packed it; it has to be in here somewhere..." She moved stuff around until her fingers found something soft and smooth.

"Wish I had thought of this earlier," she grumbled to herself as she pulled the cloak out. "We could have gotten the hammer and been back out again if I had remembered this."

She draped the cloak around her shoulders and pulled the hood up over her head, taking care to make sure that Tilson was completely covered as well. "Just be quiet, and when I stop, *don't move.*"

She slowly stepped around the corner, barely moving and keeping an eye on the beast in the lava. Whenever one of the heads turned towards her, she froze in place, feeling the sweat run down her back, in between her shoulder blades. She hoped that the sweat was just from nerves and not from the salve wearing off. She also wished that she had checked to see how much longer they had before the cream wore off and they were vulnerable to the searing heat again. When the monster turned to swim away again, she continued moving around the pool, carefully making her way to the gate.

They had almost made it all the way around the pool before Morgan's foot slipped on a patch of loose stones, sending the small rocks tumbling and echoing through the cavern.

Instantly, the creature turned, swimming at them and closing the gap far more swiftly than Morgan had expected. She stopped, motionless, and held her breath as four of the beast's heads converged directly over her, sniffing at the air over her head. Another head reared back and shrieked, a high, keening sound that reverberated in Morgan's ears and echoed off the walls of the cavern.

She felt Tilson twitch and shiver in fright behind her and hoped that his small movements would not be enough for the creature to realize where they were.

Long moments passed as the multi-headed beast sniffed the air around them before it gave up and turned back to its swimming. Afraid of a trick, Morgan remained still and silently counted the seconds for one, two, three long minutes before daring to move again.

They moved even more slowly and carefully than they had before, taking almost as long to cover the last quarter of the path as they had the previous bit, but they arrived at the gate without the monster attacking them.

Unfortunately, they discovered that the gate was not only closed but locked, too. Morgan tugged on the barrier as much as she dared but it held fast.

"Just stay here and hold really still," she heard Tilson whisper into her ear. "I might be able to open it."

Morgan nodded and Tilson slid down to the ground, his little pack in hand. He pulled a long, slim blade from the pack and climbed up the bars until he reached the lock. The blade barely fit into the keyhole but Tilson wiggled it around, worrying on the lock until it opened with a sharp click.

Again, the monster investigated the noise. Tilson dropped to the ground and rolled under the cloak so that he would not be visible out in the open. Unfortunately, the creature noticed the movement and two heads screeched and a couple more inhaled to blast them with fire.

Morgan didn't wait to see if they were still protected, or if the salve would protect them from that kind of a blast. She leaned down, scooped up the quivering haltija and ran through the gate, slamming it closed behind them. She heard the gate click as it closed but she didn't stop to check.

She ran as fast and as hard as she could to get away from the beast, taking the first turn that she came to. Even then, she didn't slow, not knowing if the click she had heard was the gate locking once more behind them. She had no idea if the creature could get through the gate, locked or unlocked, and had no intention of waiting to find out.

She ran.

Through more twists and turns than she could count, Morgan held tight to Tilson. They could hear the monster bellowing and shrieking behind them but the noise slowly faded as they got further away. After what felt like hours, Moran could run no further and had to stop.

She sank against the wall of the tunnel, panting and gasping for breath, wiping away the sweat that was running freely down her face and stinging her eyes. Her clothes were soaked and, looking down at the haltija, Morgan noticed that he was shining with sweat as well. "I think," she said, "that we have to keep going."

Tilson nodded as a drop of sweat fell from his chin and landed on Morgan's arm. "It's getting hotter in here, isn't it?"

Morgan looked at her watch to see how long they had been in the mountain, only to discover that they had been inside the mountain for over five and a half hours already. She reached into her pack, looking for the jar of salve in the hope that there was enough left to give them each a thin coating so they could survive a bit longer.

Instead, she discovered that the jar had broken at some point, either during their capture when she had been slammed into the wall, or perhaps during their escape. Everything in her pack was coated with the gel. Blinking back tears, she stood up.

This couldn't be happening, she thought to herself. They were so close.

"We're already past time and I have no idea how much longer this stuff is going to hold up.

We need to get that hammer and get out of here, now."

Tilson climbed up her arm and over her shoulder to drop into her hood and the pair continued along the tunnel. Morgan tried to hurry but her legs felt like rubber and her lungs were only just beginning to stop burning from her panicked sprint from the lava pool. She could only walk at a slow pace, her feet dragging along the ground and beads of sweat running down her back.

Eventually they came across a tunnel that appeared to lead more upwards, so she turned, hoping that going up would eventually mean a way out. Her clothes were sticking to her body, her hair was plastered to her head, and all she wanted right now was to take a deep breath of air that didn't smell of burnt matches.

She was about to give up hope of ever seeing Askel, Corran, her parents and anyone she knew ever again when Tilson perked up.

"I hear something!"

Morgan stopped to listen. "I don't hear anything."

"That's because you are a human. I have better ears, so I can hear better than you can. There's pounding up there."

Morgan picked up the pace a bit, as much as she could. Trusting in the haltija's sense of hearing, she followed his directions. After much more walking, she started to hear the faint echoes as well, sounds of metal being pounded into metal. She stopped to listen for a moment before realizing where she had heard that sound before. "It's the workshop!"

The metallic clanging that had echoed through the workshop sounded like it was directly ahead of them now. She hitched the satchel up on her shoulder and began to walk again, quickening the pace.

Sweat ran in rivers down her face, neck, and back, but Morgan didn't notice as much as she had before. The sounds of Volcan working ahead were getting closer as they moved and soon Morgan could see the flickering light of his fires. She switched off the flashlight and pulled the stifling cloak over her head once more.

Slowing down as they approached Volcan's workshop, Morgan carefully picked her way to the opening of the massive chamber and peeked inside, being cautious of her steps. She didn't want to step on any more loose stones and give themselves away when they were this close.

The light inside the chamber was blinding after all the time the pair had spent in darkness. Morgan raised a hand to shade her eyes and scanned the room for the enormous man.

Volcan was not too far away, about four tables to her left, bent over and looking closely at his work. Whoever he had been talking with had apparently left after their capture because there was no sign of him. Morgan could see something shining on the table but couldn't tell what it was. At that moment, however, she was less concerned with whatever Volcan was working on than with the location of his hammer.

She watched him work, wiping the sweat out of her eyes, until she was sure that she could move into the room past him without being detected. As soon as Volcan's back was turned, Morgan scampered as quietly as she could into the room and ducked behind a massive barrel. She peeked around the side of it and checked to make sure that they hadn't been seen.

Waiting more long minutes for Volcan to turn away from them once more, she looked over the section of the room that was in view, trying to catch a glimpse of the hammer. Not seeing it from her hiding spot, she decided to hazard another move and crept further into the room.

She snuck towards the center of the enormous chamber, dodging around blazing fires and stacks of metals in many different forms. A couple of times she dove under a table, certain that Volcan had discovered her again and was sneaking up behind her. Every time she checked, however, she discovered that the enormous smith was still at work at the far table.

Finally, she caught a glimpse of the handle of the giant hammer that she had been sent to retrieve. Only after verifying that Volcan was nowhere near the precious hammer did she move towards it, hiding under the table upon which it had been placed.

She reached out a hand and groped across the table, wincing at the quiet scraping sound the hammer made as it slid across the top of the table. She almost dropped it when she slid it clear of the table top, not realizing how heavy the enormous hammer was.

It was easily four feet long, almost as tall as she was; its head was bigger around than her thigh. She sat down on the floor under the table, trying to figure out a way of escaping with the heavy piece of metal.

She couldn't just carry it, she knew that. She would likely drop it before making it the rest of the way across the room and she didn't want to risk discovery again. The only thing she could do was to wear it like a backpack. She nodded to herself and pulled off the satchel that was still slung over her shoulder.

"You're going to have to walk the rest of the way," he quietly explained to Tilson. "There's no way I'm going to be able to carry this thing, my pack, and you too." With a curt nod, the haltija silently scampered toward the exit.

She reached into the pack and pulled out the coil of rope that Corran had given her what felt like ages ago. It was slick and foul-smelling from the salve that had broken open but it would have to work. She began to tie the rope around the hammer, making a pair of shoulder straps so that she could carry the immense tool.

Once she was sure that the hammer was secured to her back, she gathered up her pack in her arms and began to slowly creep across the cavern. Adjusting the straps to be slightly less uncomfortable, she took one last look towards the smith, who was still hard at work, and followed the haltija.

Panting with effort, she walked towards the exit that led to the outside world. To remain as unseen as possible, she hunched over and tried to keep her head low, but she knew that if Volcan looked in her direction, he couldn't help but see her.

Around barrels and tables, fires and implements that she didn't want to know their use, she hurried. The exit was close, closer, and finally she saw Tilson dart around the corner into the tunnel leading out.

She risked another glance behind her, only to discover that the giant man was no longer working at the table where he had been. Instead, he was carrying a large mound of metal towards the table that had only moments before held the hammer.

Turning away, not wanting to see what she knew would follow, she ducked around the corner into the tunnel. Once she was clear of the workshop, she took in a deep breath and exhaled a quick sigh of relief.

She knew immediately when Volcan discovered the theft. An earth-shattering bellow echoed through the tunnel, reverberating from the walls, ceiling, and Morgan swore she could feel it through her shoes as it rattled the floor beneath her. "Run!" she screamed.

Tilson needed no encouragement. He hitched his little pack more securely on his tiny shoulders and moved as fast as he could, his tail sticking almost straight out behind him for balance. Morgan couldn't move much faster than the haltija, weighed down as she was.

They ran in a panic, hearing the sounds of enormous footsteps crashing into the tunnel behind them. Volcan ran irregularly, as though he had a limp that Morgan had not previously noticed. This gave her hope that they might survive this yet, because even someone Volcan's massive size couldn't run that swiftly with a limp. Nevertheless, she didn't slow down, even once she felt the cool breeze blowing in from the outside world.

"This way," she called to Tilson as she ducked down the tunnel that she felt the fresh air coming from. There was no light ahead but that didn't slow her down.

The thunderous footsteps continued to echo behind her, and Morgan began to wonder if they would escape before Volcan caught up to them. It sounded like he was closer than he had been, limp and all. She dared a look behind her the next time she heard the deafening bellow and discovered that Volcan had turned down the same tunnel as they. She could see the gigantic man, running in his awkward gait and closing in fast.

Morgan looked forward again and discovered that they had reached the entrance of the volcanic lair. Stars were twinkling in the distance and a faint glow illuminated the exit. She ran out into the open air, relieved to feel the cool air on her face, and screamed for Askel.

"We're coming but he's right behind us!" She

fairly dove off the rock ledge and slid a number of feet on the loose dirt and stones on the mountainside. She quickly caught her balance, fear outweighing gravity, and ran further down the mountain.

She couldn't see Tilson in the dim starlight, so all she could do was pray that he had made it out safely as well. In the distance below her, she could see the shadowy form of Askel taking flight and heading towards her.

Behind her, she could hear the crashing of rocks and boulders as Volcan followed her out of the tunnel and down the hill. The huge man bellowed at her once more and Morgan's ears rang with the sound. Even though the noise was not reverberating from the walls of the tunnel, it was still very loud. Although she didn't want to look behind her to see where the behemoth was, she was fairly certain that he was close.

Askel approached closer and closer, and Morgan could hear him screech, "Jump!"

She turned towards another smaller outcropping of rocks that hung over nothing but water, far below. Without another thought, she leaped out into nothingness.

As she left the ground, she felt something huge and solid strike her leg, sending her teetering head over heels through the air. She could feel the hammer sliding around on the ropes across her back and cried out in pain as the handle slammed against the back of her legs.

Askel caught her as she fell, ripping into her shoulder with one taloned claw and halting her descent towards the water below. She cried out again but he lifted her high into the sky. He flew her up higher on the mountain, circling to find a large enough landing spot before setting her down onto the ground once more and helping her climb onto his back.

There, she found Tilson, shivering, cowering and clutching onto Askel's neck with both arms and both legs. He blinked at her as she fell onto Askel's back behind him, a mixture of fear and shock playing across his face.

Askel took off again immediately, not giving the smith a chance to catch them again. He headed out over the water, towards the rising sun.

Morgan could hardly believe that she was

alive. Her shoulder hurt terribly and she could feel blood running down the back of her arm where Askel had clawed her. Her right leg was numb from just below her hip and all the way down. Her head was still throbbing from her collision with the wall the first time that Volcan had discovered them. She wondered whether any of the painful places on her body had been broken.

She didn't care. She was alive and going home.

Safe now, she pulled the hammer from her back, being careful to not drop it into the ocean below. She held it in front of her in her lap to be sure that it was secure. Given everything that she and Tilson had just endured in order to get the tool, she wasn't interested in taking any chances with it.

After a number of hours of silent flight, Tilson started to calm down. He released his hold on Askel's neck and climbed down onto his back, settling down into his usual seat before looking back at Morgan. "You're bleeding," he whimpered.

"I know." She looked down at her shirt,

which was damp and sticky with blood. "But I can still move my arm, so it's OK." She rotated the arm at the shoulder to show him, wincing in pain as she did.

"Do you think he's gonna follow us?" Tilson looked past Morgan, towards the volcano that they had just left.

"Let's hope not." Morgan looked behind her as well, almost expecting to see Volcan coming up behind. "I don't want to deal with him again."

"Me, either. That wasn't fun." Tilson settled down on the satchel and closed his eyes. "I sure don't want to be the one that gets sent to return the stupid hammer after we're done with it."

Morgan nodded her agreement and watched as the haltija fell asleep.

They flew in a numbed sort of silence back to the council's island, speaking to each other only when necessary. Morgan slept fitfully, the pain in her shoulder and leg keeping her from getting any real rest. When the island came into view, Morgan heaved a sigh of relief and gratefully prepared to land.

Most of the council was there to meet them.

Corran stepped forward along with Arien, the man-horse with the dark brown fur and funny beard. The pair of them helped Morgan down from Askel's back and set her onto solid ground.

When they let go, however, Morgan discovered that her legs could no longer hold her weight, exhausted as she was. Her knees buckled and she would have fallen if it hadn't been for the swift movements of the fey.

Arien carried her over to a shaded area of the island and gently sat her against a tree. Without speaking, he began to examine her wounds. He poked and prodded at her shoulder, her head, and the back of her leg before backing away again. "I will return shortly. Do not move until then."

He returned a short while later, a satchel much like Morgan's slung over one shoulder. He knelt on the grass beside her, tucking his hooves beneath his body, and pulled off the satchel. From the bag, he took out a piece of wood that looked like a strip of bark. "Chew on this." He handed it to her. "It will help to ease your pain."

Doubtful but willing to try anything to make

the pain stop, Morgan put the strange bark into her mouth and chewed gently on it. The bark was bitter but not nearly as bad as biting into a lemon peel. Fairly soon, she noticed a slight tingling sensation starting at her mouth and spreading throughout her body. As the sensation spread, it dulled the pain. Morgan was amazed. "What is this?" She pulled the piece of wood from her mouth and examined it.

"It is a shaving of bark from the white willow tree," Arien responded. "It is good for easing all types of pains."

Morgan nodded and chewed on the bark some more. "Is this stuff just in the fey part of the world or do we have it too?"

"You have it too; I believe some humans use it fairly regularly." He turned back to her shoulder. "This wound needs cleaning," he said. "I will have to remove the sleeve from your shirt in order to tend it."

Morgan carefully pulled off her cloak and set it aside in the grass, knowing that it was coated in blood as well but not wanting it to be in Arien's way as he worked on her shoulder. She watched, nervously, as he pulled out a long, curved blade and slid the sharp edge against her arm.

He started at the top of her shoulder, almost at the collar, and carefully cut around her arm to release the sleeve and part of the shirt's shoulder from the rest of it. Once he finished cutting, he set the blade down on the grass next to him and peeled the sleeve away from Morgan's arm.

Red streaks marked her flesh from the top of her arm and down to her fingers. In places, the blood had pooled, leaving large maroon smudges. Morgan hadn't realized how much blood she had lost and became a bit lightheaded at the sight of the red markings. Noticing this, Arien called for another fey to bring her some water.

While Morgan sipped at the cup that was brought, Arien cleaned off the dried blood that seemed to be everywhere. Once he had removed most of the mess, both he and Morgan could see where Askel had punctured her arm as he caught her. There were a number of deep gouges from his claws and one deep hole where he had latched onto her. This largest wound was still bleeding slightly; the others had long since closed up.

Arien pulled another salve from his pack and smoothed it onto the wound. "This is not too bad," he said approvingly. "I had believed it to be far worse."

Morgan was pleased to discover that this salve was not as foul-smelling as the one that she and Tilson had used inside the volcano. It smelled more of flowers and some strange mixture of herbs that tickled her nose, but not too badly. It left a cool feeling on her arm and the pain subsided even more.

Finally free of pain, with Arien working to heal her further, Morgan fell asleep.

~ 14 ~

STORYTELLER

Morgan woke in the clearing, long after the sun had set. The twin fey moons and a couple of stars shone in the sky overhead and she was covered in a thick woolen blanket. When she moved to get up, she discovered that Tilson was there as well, tucked into the blanket next to her. She got up carefully, trying not to wake the sleeping haltija.

She wandered through the lonely darkness, remembering the first time she had been to Zea Island. She wondered how Einar was doing, now that he no longer had to guard Cinderflare's lair. She thought about Kun and Yuki-onna, the strange woman that had lured Morgan out into the snowstorm. She hoped that Kun was finally able to return to his home, wherever that had been, knowing that the giant was not fond of the frozen climate where they had met.

She thought of the Ghirtablili and wondered if it had managed to resume guarding Amahté-Baki's lair.

More than anything, she wondered if the council was right in its belief that a human was responsible for killing the dragons, and if it was a human, who it was.

She found herself wandering into the tunnel that led to Stormshock's grotto. She didn't bother to bring a flashlight but navigated by the minimal light that the moons and stars shone through the trees. As she knew she would, she found the entrance to the clearing, with the circular path leading to the rocky pool in the center.

She followed the path as it wound around and around the clearing, remembering the first time she had walked it. Although she knew that it had not been that long since she had been brought into this strange, magical world, it seemed like ages. When she reached the end of the winding path and climbed onto the rocks, she almost expected to see her old friend, lounging in the water as he always had been.

Instead, she found a boy, sitting on the rocks on the other side of the pool. He was silent, watching her as she settled onto her customary seat on the rocks.

"You must be the newest chosen that everyone's raving about." He stood and slowly approached her, walking without needing to look down at the jutting rocks beneath his feet. Somehow, Morgan thought this was not the first time that the boy had stood upon these rocks and a feeling of dread settled into the pit of her stomach. Refusing to be intimidated, she didn't get up but quietly watched the boy approach.

As he got closer, Morgan noticed that the boy was a bit older than she had first thought, possibly sixteen bur not older than twenty. He was not very tall, maybe six inches taller than Morgan, with hair that was somewhere between blond and brown. He was dressed in a red sweatshirt that was zipped up in the front and tattered jeans, ripped both at the knees and one of the front pockets. His sneakers were old and worn as well, with laces tied together in a few places where they had broken.

"I hadn't expected to see you so soon." He stopped a number of paces away from Morgan and looked at her thoughtfully. "You must be more resourceful than I'd thought to escape Volcan's lair." His gaze drifted to the water, where both of their reflections bobbed in the slight wind. "Not many could have made it out of there alive."

Morgan blinked at him, unsure of what he was getting at. "Do I know you?"

"Not really. I haven't been around much recently." He looked around the glade. "Not that much has changed much in my absence." He stepped around Morgan and surveyed the clearing.

"Is Corran still trying to lord over everyone?" He looked back at the girl. "Or has Stormshock's death actually given him the power that he wanted so much?"

"I...I don't know what you mean. He is the one in charge now, at least as far as I can tell, but he hasn't been acting lordly." She turned to face the boy. "At least, not that I have seen."

"Odd. I had thought you must have been around for longer, considering how much work they've been giving you." He smiled to himself and shook his head slightly. "You must still be new, though." He turned back to the glade again. "It usually takes a little while for a new chosen to realize how self-serving most of the elvor are." He paced back and forth on the stones, apparently deep in thought.

As Morgan watched him pace, the wind picked up, carrying a sound that she hadn't heard before, a high, shrill keening, too high to be just the breeze whistling through the trees. Although she could tell that the sound came from a distance away, it was still loud enough to make her want to cover her ears.

As the sound continued, Morgan started to feel a deep sadness welling up deep inside her, as though her heart was breaking over and over again, without any time to heal in between. She tried to lift her hands up to block the sound, but found moving to be difficult. Slowly, she sank to the ground and listened, watching the boy through a teary blur.

The boy was affected by the sound as well, Morgan could tell. Tears ran down his cheeks and dripped unnoticed onto the rocks. He stood facing the sound and spoke in a low voice. To Morgan, it sounded like he was apologizing for something.

After far too long for Morgan's comfort, the sound faded. Slowly, she reached up and dried her tears on the sleeve of her sweater, once she no longer felt the overwhelming sense of sorrow.

"She's unhappy." The boy turned back towards Morgan. "I don't expect you to understand. In fact, I'm surprised you're reacting to her at all." He turned and jumped off the rocks, landing on the grass below. "And for what they've done to her, to us, I can never forgive them." He headed off towards the exit.

Morgan started to get to her feet, to follow him and find out who he was and what he meant, but by the time she reached the opening to the tunnel leading out of Stormshock's meadow, the boy was gone. She followed the dark tunnel, expecting to come across him at any moment, but there was no sign of him.

Regretfully, she stepped out of the tunnel and discovered her friends were still asleep. Only now realizing that the wounds on her arm and leg were aching, she headed over to her satchel to pull out one of the pieces of bark that Arien had left for her. As she chewed, she sat and watched the sun come up over the trees, wondering about the strange encounter she had just experienced.

Before she had too much time to puzzle over the morning's events, a figure came walking out from between a couple of the trees that surrounded the clearing. Morgan pushed herself to her feet, grabbing up her staff in the process.

"Ah, I see you are awake." Corran stepped further into the light, heading for Morgan. "Arien should be here shortly to check on your wounds." As he got closer, he noticed what Morgan was chewing on and paused. "Are you in pain? I can call for him to arrive sooner if it is needed."

Morgan shook her head. "They only started hurting a couple minutes ago but it's not bad, really." Realizing that she was still holding it out in front of her, she lowered her staff.

"Are you certain that you are all right?" Corran took a couple more steps towards her to scrutinize her more closely. "You don't look well, not at all. Perhaps you should rest a bit more." He helped her back to a seated position and went to find a cup of water for her, which he held for her to drink.

"You didn't look this ill when we left you last night. Has something happened?"

Morgan took a couple of swallows from the cup before responding, trying to sort her thoughts and decide which part to explain first. "There was a... a sound, a few minutes ago. I'm not sure what it was."

Corran nodded and sat down next to her, crossing his legs in front of him and resting the cup in the junction of his ankles. "We weren't sure if you would be able to sense that or not. Most humans cannot hear her wail until they have been among us for a much longer time than you have."

"What was it?"

The elvor looked down at the cup, and an

expression crossed his face, one that Morgan hadn't expected to see on him. She wasn't sure if it was sadness, anger, or some mixture of both.

"That wasn't a what, but a whom. Her name was Avekaine and she used to be an elvor."

"Used to be? I don't understand." Morgan looked around, almost expecting to hear the sound again, but the clearing was silent. "Does that mean that she's dead?"

"Almost." Corran stood up, much more quickly than Morgan had expected him to be able. He paced back and forth in front of her, not seeming to realize that he was passing the cup of water back and forth, from one hand to the other.

"How can someone be almost dead?" Morgan watched him pace, growing more worried as he moved. She couldn't understand how anyone, human or fey, could be *almost* dead. Dead was just one of those things that you either were or weren't.

"For all intents and purposes, yes, she is dead. The difference is that when she passed, something went wrong and we aren't sure what. Her ethereal essence, her soul, whatever you want to call it, was never released back into the fabric of the world." He stopped pacing and looked down at the sitting girl.

"Not like the ether trapped in the spheres, this is a natural occurrence. It is rare but it has been known to happen on occasion. I just don't know why, or what causes it." He closed his eyes and took a deep breath before continuing. "The elders spoke of them a couple of times, they called them cyhyraeth." He looked at Morgan once more. "I believe you have legends about them in the human world; you just have a different name for them."

Noticing the cup in his hands, he looked deep into the water. "The humans call them the banshee."

Morgan blinked at him. She had heard of a banshee but she couldn't really remember what it was or if they were supposed to be good or bad. She really hoped that they were good, but remembering the overwhelming feeling of sadness that the sound had made in her, she shivered. Even if the cyhyraeth were good, she wanted no part of them.

"Cyhyraeth are quite uncomfortable to hear. I believe that may be the reason that you are looking as worn out as you are." Morgan hadn't noticed, but at some point, Arien had arrived to join the conversation. He settled down next to her, tucked his hooves beneath him, and set a small plate of food on her lap.

"Eat this. It will calm your stomach and help you to recover from the effects of her wail."

Morgan looked down at the plate. There were a couple of breads, although they were a bit darker in color than she was used to, and some sort of paste that she couldn't identify. Hesitantly, she scooped up some of the paste and tried it. "It's delicious!" She smiled over at Arien and used the bread to scoop up the fruit-flavored paste. The bread tasted a lot richer than she was used to but it tasted heavenly.

As she ate, Arien looked over her injuries. "You seem to be healing nicely but I believe that you should continue to rest for a couple more days, at the least." He looked over at Corran. "Have you sent someone to her home as she is recuperating?"

Corran nodded. "Liore has been there the

whole time. I will send word to her so that she knows she will be there a little bit longer." He turned and walked out of sight.

Morgan watched the elvor leave and then turned back to Arien. "I have a couple of questions, if you don't mind me asking."

Arien made himself more comfortable next to her and nodded. "Of course you may ask, and I will do my best to answer."

"Okay." Morgan finished off the last of the fruit paste before beginning. "First, and I'm not sure if this is offensive or not, so I hope it isn't." She looked up at the horse-man a bit sheepishly. "We have tales about something like you back home but you fey all seem to call yourselves something different than what I know. I think you might be a centaur but I'm not really sure. Are you?"

Arien chuckled before responding. "You are close. I am an apotharni. We are rather closely related to the centaurs but where they are part horse, we are part goat. There are no centaurs in this area, which is really for the best." He took her now-empty plate and set it on the grass beside him. "Bloodthirsty creatures, really. Not only do centaurs eat only meat, they prefer to eat it while it is still alive." He shuddered a bit at the thought.

"Wow, umm...okay." Morgan sat back a bit at that proclamation.

"You have more questions? Or do you wish to wait for a while?"

"No, I am all right." She thought for a moment before speaking again. "Before Corran and you got here, I went for a walk and I ended up at Stormshock's grotto. There was a boy there who seemed to know you guys pretty well. Is he a chosen, too?"

"I am not sure I understand." Arien looked around the glade. "Was this a dream?"

"No, it was earlier this morning. I woke up and wanted to go for a walk and I ended up on the other side of the tunnel. When I went up to sit by the pool, there he was." She looked up at Arien's face, not sure that he understood her. "We talked for a couple of minutes but when the cyhyraeth started moaning, he left. I tried to follow him but he was gone by the time I came back out of the tunnel."

"You must be mistaken. That tunnel has

been sealed for some time now. You could not have possibly been inside it today."

"No, I'm sure of it. I was there just this morning." Morgan climbed to her feet and walked across the grass, heading for the entrance to the tunnel. Arien followed, saying nothing.

On the other side of the clearing, Morgan began to circle around at the tree line, looking for the entrance to the tunnel. She was certain that it had to be there; she remembered it clearly. "It was here, I know it was."

Corran joined them as they circled the clearing, looking towards Arien with a quizzical look.

"She believes that she was at Stormshock's grotto this morn, before you or I arrived."

"That's not possible; it has been sealed." Corran hastened his steps to catch up with Morgan. "While you were delivering the sphere to Magicgleam, the council sealed the entrance. It is simply not there anymore." He tried to lay a hand on Morgan to calm her down but she shrugged it off. "It had to have been a dream."

"It wasn't a dream and I'm going to show you." She turned around as they approached Askel's still-sleeping form and headed back around the circle once more. "It was real, I was there and I spoke to someone in there. I wasn't asleep. I was just as awake as I am right now."

Arien and Corran talked to her, trying to explain that what she remembered couldn't possibly have been real, until Morgan stopped abruptly and pointed to the ground. "See! I told you I wasn't dreaming."

The fey stopped as well, looking down at the grass where she was pointing. Just inside the trees, where the ground was still damp from the morning dew, was a small footprint. It perfectly matched the ones beneath Morgan's feet.

They followed the footprints deeper into the woods, where they stopped. Corran looked over at Arien. "This is where his tunnel was."

"Could these have been from before the entrance was removed?"

"No, they are fresh." Corran knelt to the ground next to the last print. "And they stop here, which is where she would have entered the tunnel."

"But how? The tunnel hasn't been there for days; she couldn't have gone through."

"I am not sure." Corran stood back up. "I

will speak with the rest of the council regarding this. If someone did manage to reopen the tunnel, even for a short period of time, they need to know."

Looking from Morgan to Arien, he continued. "Perhaps they may be able to find the source of the magic that did this. Until then, we should leave this be."

Later that afternoon, after the excitement of the morning had calmed down and Corran had left to confer with the rest of the council, Morgan sat with Arien once more.

"Why was Corran so upset when I mentioned hearing the cyhyraeth?"

Arien sighed. "That is a long story." He took a moment to gather his thoughts while Morgan got more comfortable. "Had he mentioned that a cyhyraeth is a creature that was once an elvor?" When Morgan nodded, he continued.

"The cyhyraeth was once an elvor named Avekaine. She was a quiet one, generally keeping to herself and not running and playing as much as the other elvor children did. Avekaine's mother, Corran's sister, was quite worried about the child so she sent her daughter to live among us, fearing that she was afflicted with some sort of illness."

"Was she?"

"No," Arien smiled. "She wasn't. After she had been here for a number of years, she began to open up, to smile and laugh. Everyone thought that the council's influence was the reason for her improvement but that was not the case. Corran spoke with her quite a lot during this time and discovered that the reason for the change in her behavior was not because of her time with the council, but because she had developed a bond with another here."

"So it wasn't because of the council, but one of the council members?"

"That was also what we believed. Corran was practically beside himself, trying to figure out to whom she had grown so attached but was not able to determine who." He paused again, reflecting. "After a while, Corran and the rest of the council decided that, no matter what the reason, she had changed into a much happier elvor. They let her be, keeping an eye on her from a distance."

"She had also grown up quite a lot during

this time and eventually her parents decided that she was ready to lifemate with another."

Morgan interrupted. "What's that?"

"When an elvor, like many of the other fey, come of age to start their own family, their parents begin to discuss among the other elvor families to find a suitable mate for their children. Sometimes families are able to decide while the children are still young but at other times, the decision is not made until much later. When a suitable mate is found and both families are agreed, the children are brought together. I am not certain of the elvor ceremony, as I have not attended one, but after the pair of children has been lifemated, they are able to start their own family and have children of their own."

"So it's like an arranged marriage, then."

"Quite a bit, yes."

"Was she lifemated to her friend in the council?"

"No, she was not. Although her parents had been informed that she was very close to someone here, it was not known who it was, at least not then. Because of that, they could not arrange with the family of the one she wished to be lifemated with. Instead, they made arrangements with another family from the area they had originally come from."

Arien paused again. "Quite a nice young elvor, as I remember. Not overly loud but pleasant enough. I cannot recall his name, however."

Morgan understood what the young elvor must have been feeling at the news. "She couldn't have been too happy about that, being taken from here and her friends."

"No, she was not pleased at all. In fact, she refused to leave with her family when they came to retrieve her. Corran had to help his sister remove her from the island and take her back home. I had never heard that little girl kick up as much of a fuss as she did on that day. I don't think that anyone else here was expecting it, either. She fought them all, kicking, hitting, and screaming at everyone. Had she been much stronger, she might have even managed to release herself of them."

"That's awful!" Morgan tried to imagine what it must have been like to be forcibly torn away like that. She shuddered. "No wonder she didn't want to go."

Arien nodded. "Many of us who were here that day were appalled and felt that the girl should remain, to be released back to her family under less stressful circumstances. But her family wished to have her lifemated by the end of the summer and didn't believe that she would be any more reasonable by then."

"Corran returned about a week later, in a terrible ire. Apparently, Avekaine had fought the entire journey and then refused to be lifemated, unless it was to the man of her choosing. Although her parents were not pleased with this, they agreed to consider her choice but refused as soon as they discovered who it was."

Morgan was leaned forward, listening intently to Arien's story. "Who was it?"

"We didn't know, not then. I am sure that Corran knew but he wouldn't say. All he told us was that Avekaine's parents had refused her request and that she was lifemated to the elvor that her parents had chosen for her."

"That's horrible! How could they do that to her?"

Arien nodded. "We thought much the same.

I even asked Corran about his sister's decision but he refused to speak of it."

"Did you ever find out who it was that she had wanted instead?"

Arien nodded again. "We did, although not until some time later." He stopped speaking and took a few deep breaths. "We had a chosen then, much like you are, although the times were not as immediately dangerous as they are now. He was a bright young lad named Leander.

"Leander had been our chosen for a number of years and Corran insisted that it was time for him to be returned to his world as well. We were used to this; sometimes those chosen to work with us turned out to not be able to handle it for long, although some excel at it and don't want to leave our world for their own as they grow older."

"Like the druids I met with earlier."

"Exactly," Arien nodded. "Although Leander was not quite to the age that our chosen normally return to the human world, Corran insisted that he was not doing well and talked the council into sending him home early.

"Of course, Leander insisted that he was fine,

that he did not need to be released early, but once the council decides, it is a difficult thing to change their minds."

"Furthermore, and this always seemed a bit strange to me, Corran also insisted that the boy needed to keep no memories of us and his time among us. His explanation was that, because Leander was so insistent that he could continue for longer, Corran was concerned that he might try to return to us, possibly leading others to us as well. The council agreed that they could not take that risk and so the boy was returned home with no memories of us or all that he had been doing over the last number of years."

Morgan blinked. "The one that Avekaine had wanted to be lifemated with was Leander? The chosen?"

Arien nodded. "It was, although we did not realize this for some time, far too long to mend any of the damage that had been done. Avekaine was never allowed back to the council island again and she never knew that Leander had been returned to the world of humans. At least, not at first."

"What happened?"

"I am not certain exactly what happened. A number of years passed and the council decided that it was best to just move on and leave the whole episode behind. Avekaine had been life-mated and had settled down, not entirely happy but not in any danger that we knew of. Leander settled back into his life among the humans and those sent to watch over him reported that he had adjusted well, so all was as it should be. A new chosen was found and life continued."

"So the council knew what had happened?"

"As I said, not at first. As time went on, more and more fey discovered the truth. Corran insisted that this had to be kept quiet, to keep his family from embarrassment and to keep the council from embarrassment as well. They all agreed and it was not spoken of after. To this day, it is not openly discussed."

"But what about Avekaine? How did she become a cyhyraeth?"

"At some point, she must have discovered what had happened to Leander. Corran started to receive messages from her, very angry messages. She believed that Leander should be reinstated with the council. Corran of course refused, saying that so many years had passed that Leander was beyond the age of believing. They argued over this, until one day the messages stopped."

"Corran was relieved that she had finally come to her senses, that is, until his sister came to see him. She was in a terrible state, far more agitated than I had ever seen her, and it was obvious that she had spent the entire journey in tears. She took Corran away with her and when he returned, we discovered what had happened.

"Apparently Avekaine had been so distraught over all that had happened that she threw herself from the cliffs near her new home."

"And Leander never knew?"

"We had believed not but that may no longer be the case."

"What do you mean?"

He turned to face Morgan more fully. "The description of the person you saw at Stormshock's grotto sounds just like Leander."

~ 15 ~

LEANDER

Morgan stayed with the fey in the clearing for two more weeks, talking with Arien and Corran while she healed. Corran did not wish to discuss Avekaine and soon Morgan stopped trying to ask about her.

More members of the council arrived and spent most of their time trying to determine if and how the entrance to Stormshock's lair had been opened and closed again. After a few days of discussing and arguing amongst themselves, they came to the conclusion that only a very powerful magus could have opened the portal, for they all agreed that it had indeed been opened.

Morgan felt a bit vindicated at this but also a bit worried. If the boy at the pool had been Leander and he was the one that had opened the portal, how had he done it? And how had he remembered about the fey in the first place, if his memories of them had been removed? She tried to ask Corran but, as usual, he didn't want to discuss it. She tried to ask Arien but he didn't have any answers. She tried to ask Tilson but he didn't care.

"I don't know why you keep harping on that anyway; you are supposed to be healing so we can both get back home. I am stuck here for as long as you are here, you know, and I have better things to be doing than sitting around like this."

"Arien said I would probably be able to go home either tomorrow or the day after, so calm down. I don't really like being stuck here, either. Besides, I don't really see what you're complaining so much about; you aren't the one that got hurt!"

"Didn't get hurt? What do you mean I didn't

get hurt?" Tilson picked up his tail and held the end out towards her. The fur at the tip had gotten singed and was a bit crispy at the ends. "My poor tail! I don't know if it's going to recover or not." He sat back down and cradled his tail on his lap. "We spent two days inside a volcano and she says I didn't get hurt. I still don't know why I was sent into that nightmare in the first place."

"It wasn't two days; it wasn't even one day."

"Felt like two days." Tilson sniffled. "Heck, it felt like a week."

Morgan sat down next to him, picked him up, and placed him into her lap where she could smooth his fur. "I'm sorry. I know all of this hasn't been easy for you, either."

"Of course it hasn't. I was just supposed to go fetch you and bring you to the council when they needed you. I am just a guide, that's all, not a warrior to be sent out to die." The haltija sniffed, and wiped his face with one furry paw. "I don't want to do this anymore."

He jumped out of her lap and ran over to the other side of the glade, leaving Morgan to sit and think, alone. She watched as he disappeared into the bushes and wondered if he really meant that he wasn't coming back. She hoped not. For all of his complaining, she had grown quite attached to the haltija.

As the sun began to set that evening, Arien came over to check on her again. He looked over the injuries to her leg and her shoulder, pronouncing them to be healed enough for her to travel in the morning. "Liore has been at your house, covering for you in your absence, so I am certain that there hasn't been too much trouble while you were gone. Corran has been getting reports from her, and she hasn't mentioned anything too terrible."

"So I'm going home now?"

"Not exactly. Corran and Magicgleam have been discussing how best to use the hammer and they decided that the hammer should be brought to her lair. I agree with them that it will be much easier to transport the hammer than all of the spheres that have been collected. Since you are almost healed, you may be allowed to accompany them to deliver the hammer tomorrow if you wish. Once that is finished, you will be able to return to your home."

That night, Morgan slept fitfully, curled up

next to Askel. She had grown accustomed to having Tilson there as well, trying to steal her blanket, but he didn't show up. In the morning, as she gathered her things together for the trip back home, she looked around the glade, hoping to see him darting around in the grass as he usually did. There was no sign of him.

In the morning, they set out for Halkirk Island. Morgan climbed onto Askel's back, making sure to have enough room for the haltija in case he decided to come along, but he didn't show. Askel turned back to look at her after she was settled onto his back "Where is Tilson?"

"I don't think he's coming."

"Why not?"

"He decided that all of this was too dangerous for him and he doesn't want to do it anymore. At least," she took one last look across the clearing as Askel prepared to leave, "that was what he said last night."

As they took off and Askel leaped into the sky, Morgan kept her eyes on the field, hoping to see one last sight of her friend, to no avail.

"Maybe he will change his mind," Askel tried to reassure her.

"Maybe." Morgan just shrugged. "But I doubt it. He was really scared."

Corran rode another gryphon, this one with black fur and dark brown feathers. He had Volcan's hammer fastened securely before him. They flew for most of the day but Morgan hardly noticed. Her mind kept wandering back to the last time that she had been here. Tilson had been with her that time and Morgan felt his absence keenly. She leaned forward on Askel's back and closed her eyes against the blustering wind.

She wasn't able to rest for long. The Amulet of Kinship, long-forgotten beneath her shirt, began to vibrate. Still groggy with exhaustion, she figured that the wind was causing the necklace to rattle and went back to sleep.

With a cry of alarm, Askel fairly dropped out from underneath her and Morgan threw herself forward and grabbed a handful of feathers to maintain her hold on the gryphon. She clenched her legs against his side as she looked around to see what the problem was.

Flying next to them, she saw the same boy that had been at Stormshock's pool, the one that Arien had called Leander. He was dressed the same except for a strange necklace that Morgan hadn't noticed before. She probably wouldn't have noticed it now, except that it was glowing a fierce blue. She looked down and noticed that Leander was not riding on anything; he was flying on his own.

Morgan had only a moment to wonder if the strange necklace had something to do with it when a yelp came from Corran and her thoughts were cut short. "Morgan, get down!"

Too late, she remembered the boy's strange comments from the previous night. "Corran, Look out!"

Leander had pointed his hand towards them, and with an unintelligible shout, lines of red fire shot from each of his fingertips. The fire barely passed over Morgan's head as she ducked, she could feel the warmth as it singed her hair.

Corran wasn't so lucky. The fire hit him squarely in the chest and he slumped over his gryphon. From her perch on Askel, Morgan could hear his hiss of pain. Corran's gryphon dove towards the ground, far below them, Corran clutching to its back. Leander dove after them, preparing to fire more of the bolts.

"No!" Morgan howled, and Askel turned to intercept him. Morgan pulled out her staff, holding it tightly in both hands. She reached out to swipe at Leander but the boy deflected the blow with his free arm.

"You stay out of this, chosen. It is Corran I want." He turned slightly to fly past Morgan and Askel.

In desperation, knowing that Corran was injured badly and possibly dying, Morgan swiped at Leander again. She wasn't going to let Leander get to Corran.

He caught the staff this time, not letting it slide off his arm as he had before. He looked up at the girl, his eyes filled with rage. "I should've taken care of you when I had the chance. I had no idea that you were going to be this much of a problem. I assure you, I won't make that mistake again."

Morgan remembered being in Volcan's workroom and hearing him speaking to someone she couldn't see. Only now did she realize that Leander had anticipated their movements and set the trap for them, even warning Volcan that they were coming. "Why are you doing this?"

"Why?" Leander called back, incredulous. "Why are you helping them? Do you have any idea what they're really like? That they'll discard you as soon as you do anything that they disapprove of, no matter how large or small? They're all so drunk with their imagined power that they think they are the rulers of the world, both theirs and ours. Someone needs to stop it and I'm going to." He released his hold on her staff and turned after Corran once more.

Almost without hope, knowing that he was already too far away for her to land a solid hit, she swung the staff once more, willing it to connect.

The staff barely grazed Leander, sliding up his shoulder and around to the back of his neck, where it snagged. Morgan lost her grip and her hands slipped down from where she was holding her staff but managed to catch the very end, holding on with all of her might. With a sharp snick, the tension released and Leander plummeted away from her, straight towards the ground. Morgan watched him fall but turned away at the last moment, not wanting to watch the impact.

She pulled the staff back in and noticed something glinting at the end of it. In her panic, she had somehow activated the hook and grabbed Leander's necklace. As she pulled the chain off the end, she spotted Corran and his gryphon rising to meet with them again.

Corran was pale and not looking at all well, most of his shirt had burned completely off but his first concern was for Morgan. "Are you all right?"

"Yes, we're fine. How about you?" Morgan looked down to where Leander had landed. "He was after you, not me."

"It was more of a glancing wound than anything. My shirt took the worst of it."

"Are you sure? Do you need to turn around? We can have Arien take a look at you and maybe try again later."

"No need, we are almost there already." He pointed ahead, where Morgan could see the rock-strewn hillside in the distance. "We will land shortly and I will feel much better once we are on the ground." He visibly shivered. "Never did like flying."

Askel snorted and even Morgan had to chuckle.

Eventually they landed in the meadow that Morgan, Askel and Tilson had been to before, near the pile of colossal boulders. Morgan slid off of Askel's back and went over to help Corran down as well. Corran winced in pain as she held him up and Morgan noticed that his chest was no longer the shining golden color as the rest of his skin but was now an angry, blackened yellow. Now that she had time to look, the rest of his skin looked a bit dull as well.

"Are you sure you're all right?"

The elvor nodded. "I have a small flask in my satchel, up next to the hammer. Would you be kind enough to get that for me?"

Morgan retrieved his flask and helped him stand as he took a drink. Within seconds, his skin turned back to its normal golden hue and he was able to stand on his own once again. He recapped the flask and tucked it into a pocket of his pants.

After that, he walked over to the gryphon he

had been riding on to check him over. Once he verified that his mount hadn't been injured, he led the group over to the stone walkway that led to Magicgleam's lair.

Corran reminded them all not to stray from the path and everyone made it to the stairs at the far end. Morgan wasn't sure how Corran would fare with the stairs but he seemed to become steadier on his feet the further they went. At the bottom of the stone steps, Morgan, Askel and Corran's gryphon followed Corran into Magicgleam's chamber.

As she had last time, Morgan mistook Magicgleam's huge form for the opposite wall but Corran made no such mistake. He walked halfway into the chamber, stopped, and bowed deeply, with no sign that he had been injured other than his missing shirt. "It is a pleasure to see you again. It has been far too long."

"It has indeed, speaker of the council. I trust that you have been well?"

"Well enough." Corran straightened and looked up at the immense dragon. "As promised, we have brought the hammer of Volcan."

Magicgleam leaned down to have a better look at the hammer, which was still strapped to the gryphon. "I hear you had a bit of difficulty obtaining it. Is this correct?" She looked up from the hammer and over to Morgan.

"It was...rough," Morgan admitted. "But we made it out all right."

"Indeed you did, even with the interference of the human."

Morgan gaped at her. "You knew about that?"

"I have been updated on these occurrences by the council. I have been keeping an eye on you, and I am very sorry about your little friend."

She turned back to Corran. "I do not believe that you are well enough to wield the hammer, are you?" When the elvor shook his head, Magicgleam nodded. "I thought not. Therefore, I have brought someone of more physical strength and size to wield the hammer on our behalf."

"Are you sure that's wise? The council agreed that nobody outside the council proper should know of this."

"Of course I am certain. I have no intention of turning the hammer over to just anybody." She turned away from them and headed down a tunnel that had been out of sight behind her. "Follow me."

She led the group deeper into her cavern and down a steep tunnel that was barely large enough for her to maneuver her massive girth through. The bottom of the tunnel opened up into another cavern, almost as large as the one above had been.

In the center of the room sat the spheres. In every color of the rainbow, both dark and light, they glinted. Morgan stood in awe at the sheer number of them. "I didn't think I'd collected that many of them."

"Of course not, child," Magicgleam responded. "You didn't really think that you were the only one sent out to retrieve them, did you?"

Morgan shook her head, still shocked at the pile of globes that Magicgleam had been guarding. The pile stood over five feet high and was almost double that across. Realizing that these were all that was left of a great many dragons,

Morgan felt tears welling up in her eyes. "Are there any other dragons left, or did he get them all?"

"There are precious few dragons that managed to escape his hunt, yet some do remain." Magicgleam's voice was surprisingly gentle.

Morgan stepped closer and was able to identify Stormshock's sphere, shimmering near the top of the pile. "There are so many. How could he have done this?"

If anyone answered, Morgan didn't hear them. She stood, weeping, in the center of the room, knowing that soon her friend would be gone forever. "Why did this happen? How could anyone do this to them? I just don't understand." She sank to her knees.

Askel came up next to her and nuzzled her shoulder with his beak. He settled down beside her and wrapped a wing around the sobbing girl, doing his best to console her.

Corran gave her a few moments to calm down before coming forward to help her to her feet. "We must step back; you don't want to be too close."

Morgan let the elvor guide her away from

the pile of spheres. She watched as Magicgleam let out a shrill whistle and another fey, short and stocky, came up from yet another tunnel.

"Einar!" Morgan was surprised to see him.

"Well, if it don't be the chosen. Hadn't expected to be seein' you again so soon."

Morgan could have sat and spoken with Einar for hours about all that had happened since last she saw him but a low growl from Magicgleam caused him to turn back to the business at hand.

"Eh? What's that? The hammer's here, hmm? Well, let's come and have a look."

Corran unstrapped the hammer from his gryphon and handed it over. The dvergar took it gingerly, almost reverently and looked it over. "And this was Volcan's own, wasn't it? Mighty fine working, that it is."

He carried the hammer towards the mountain of orbs and pulled a sphere from the pile. He set it on a large, flat chunk of stone and stepped back. Everyone was silent as he took the first swing. With barely a grunt of effort, he swung the enormous hammer and slammed it down.

A blast of pressure erupted from the sphere and a swirling fog of raw magical energy enveloped the room, with lightning bolts of static chasing through the fog. The raw magic cascaded across the room, up the walls, and rained back down upon the group, like a tidal wave had just broken over them.

The ether continued raining down over them and splashing up the walls until, slowly, it faded. Morgan felt as though she had just been sent through the dryer without any fabric softener sheet. She sat there in shock for a number of long minutes after the magic had receded, staring around in shock.

"Is everyone all right?"

Morgan could hear Corran's voice through the haze the magic had left inside her head and she turned to see him. Noticing the look of concern on his face, she nodded, coughing slightly. "Was that expected?"

Corran shook his head. "I am not certain that any of us knew what to expect with this. Had we known it would be a blast like that, we likely would have chosen a more open area to release them." He turned his attention to the stocky fey, who was busily pulling another sphere from the pile. "A moment to recover, if you would."

"Perhaps it is best that you return to your island." Magicgleam leaned down towards Corran and Morgan. "I believe we can handle it from here."

Corran nodded and Askel snorted in assent. The four visitors headed back up the tunnel to the main chamber, up the stairs, and back out into the sunlight. As they stepped onto the dais, they felt another wave of magical energy. This was not as strong as it had been while they were standing in the same room but Morgan could still feel her hair trying to stand on end.

Once they left the platform, Corran and Morgan silently climbed back atop the gryphons and flew off once more.

~ 16 ~

HOMECOMING

They flew over familiar ground towards Morgan's house, landing in the back yard just inside the tree line. Morgan slipped her satchel over her shoulder, grabbed hold of her staff, and slid off of the gryphon. Before heading into the house, she turned back to him and wrapped her arms around his neck, burying her face in his soft feathers. "Is Tilson going to come back?"

"I don't know." Askel reached forward one massive wing to wrap around the girl. "But I am sure that we will see him again. And I also know that he realizes we will be there for him, should he need us."

Morgan nodded and pulled away, wiping the tears from her cheeks. "How will I know when the council needs me again?" She looked over at Corran, who had landed a short distance away from them.

"I am not sure yet, but we will figure out a way of contacting you." He looked back up towards the house. "You had best get inside; it is starting to grow cold."

Morgan nodded and regretfully headed up to her house. She didn't look back when Askel and Corran left but she could hear the gryphons running down the side of the hill as they prepared to take flight. She trudged up the steps to the back door and let herself inside.

Her house was as she remembered it. The kitchen was clean, with a bowl of fruit that her mother always had out on the counter. Morgan stopped to grab an apple and ate it, feeling almost like an intruder in her own home. So much had happened since the last time she had been in these rooms. Before she finished the apple, she headed deeper into the house.

In the living room, there was a new magazine on the coffee table, one of those cooking and house decorating magazines that her mother was always buying but which Morgan didn't understand at all. She sat on the couch and flipped through it regardless. She took a couple more bites of her apple, dropped the magazine back onto the table, and headed upstairs to her room.

In her room, she gaped at the mess. Fast-food wrappers were everywhere, clothes were scattered across the bed, floor, and her chair. Wadded-up balls of paper were everywhere except in the trash can and movie and video game disks were placed on every flat and almost-flat surface in the room. Morgan went to put her satchel and staff in her closet and noticed that there weren't very many clean clothes left in it. As she dropped the satchel onto the floor, she heard a noise from behind her.

Liore had walked in behind her and stood in the doorway, looking shocked at Morgan's ragged appearance. She had apparently just gotten back from school because she was still carrying Morgan's backpack. "Are you all right?" She set the pack on the floor just inside the door and stepped closer to Morgan. "What happened to you?"

Morgan just sighed. "I'll tell you soon, but I need a shower first." She indicated the clothes that were in the closet. "Is this all the clean stuff that's left?"

Liore looked sheepish. "I had thought I would have enough time to get this mess cleaned up and wash up some laundry before you got back."

"No worries." Morgan pulled a dress out of the closet. "Right now, I don't really care how much of a mess it is in here; I just want to go clean up."

She turned the shower on as hot as she could handle and stepped in, watching the steam rise across the room. As it swirled around, it reminded her of the ether that was released with every swing Einar made with the hammer, bringing a fresh bout of tears to her eyes.

Most of the sticky, slimy salve that she and Tilson had used in the volcano had worn off or been absorbed into the skin, but in places she could still smell it. The odor of the salve blended with the herbal ointment that Arien had used to treat her wounds after returning to the council's island.

She looked over the puncture marks on her arm, which had not yet fully healed and wondered how she was going to hide these from her mother. Although they didn't look nearly as bad as they had just a couple of days ago, they were still quite red and a little swollen. At least they didn't hurt anymore but she had a couple strips of bark in case they started to ache again.

She needed to wash her hair three times just to get all of the sweat and salve smell out of it. Finally, she turned off the water and stepped out of the tub to dry off.

After getting dressed again, she went back into her room, where she discovered Liore had made some progress in cleaning up the mess that had coated it earlier. All of the trash was in the trash can and piles of dirty laundry were sorted across the floor. Morgan picked up the pile that had her favorite pair of jeans in it and headed downstairs to the laundry room.

Her mother was in her office, arguing with someone on the phone. She was explaining that someone had already filed for a patent on one of her client's inventions and, if they didn't contest it soon, her client would lose the patent rights. Morgan thought about looking in to see which invention it was but decided against it. Instead, she went back upstairs.

Liore, back in her natural form, sat on the edge of Morgan's bed. "Corran said that you were having a rough time out there."

Morgan nodded. She explained to the elvor about all that had happened while she was out, and about all of the strange and amazing things she had seen and done. She told her about how scared she had been in the volcano, being chased by the angry giant. As she talked, her voice cracked and she sniffed to hold back the flood of tears that she barely had under control. Liore reached out to wrap her arms around her, pulling her in tight.

A tear spilled down her cheek as she explained that Tilson had decided not to be a part of it anymore.

Morgan let Liore hold her for a few minutes before pulling back and wiping her face. "I did it, though."

"What?"

"I did it. I did it all. I flew on a gryphon. I found a lot of the spheres; even if I wasn't the only one looking, I know I found a lot. I met with the last of the Ancients and solved her riddle. I slept in a pyramid. I survived inside a volcano for almost six hours, an hour longer than I was supposed to. I even hit Leander with my staff when he was attacking Corran. I knocked him out of the air."

Morgan stopped talking and looked out the window, where a few birds were chasing each other across the sky. "I just wish it had happened earlier so that Stormshock could have survived."

"I know." The elvor reached out to smooth Morgan's hair. "Just know that he is proud of you. We all are. We owe you our lives, you know."

Morgan thought about this for a moment. "I guess I never really thought about that. I got all caught up in what I was doing and pretty much forgot about *why* I was doing it."

"That happens a lot, especially when a chosen is still new."

"So what happens next?" Morgan looked up to meet the elvor's eyes. "Do I just go back to being a normal human and pretend this never happened?"

"Of course not. You are a chosen." Liore smiled at the girl. "I am certain that Corran will send for you again soon enough."

Liore stood up and headed for the window. "I have to go, although I would love to sit and talk with you more. However, I want you to remember one thing." Her usually smiling face became serious at this. "Be careful. Just because you didn't let Leander get Corran, that doesn't mean he won't try again. He was plenty angry when he was sent back to the human world."

"But he's dead. Nobody could have survived that fall."

Liore shook her head. "Did you actually see him hit the ground?" When Morgan shook her head in response, Liore continued. "If he had enough magical skill to trap the ether in those spheres like he did, he isn't very likely to have been taken out by a little fall, now is he?"

Morgan's eyes widened. "I didn't actually see him hit the ground. I...I looked away."

The elvor nodded. "I am sure that he had some sort of a backup plan. He always was a smart one." She looked out the window again and back to the girl. "I am serious, be careful. He knows who you are now and if you stopped him from getting Corran like he wanted, he isn't going to forgive you for that anytime soon."

"So what do I do?"

"Just keep your eyes open and watch for him. You know what to look for now. Keep wearing the amulet that Tellius gave you. You may need it."

Once Liore disappeared out the window, Morgan sat and thought about what the fey had said. She hadn't considered that Leander might have survived the fall. She took a furtive look around the room, just in case, but didn't notice anything amiss. Nevertheless, she opened the closet and dug through her satchel. Pulling out the amulet, she dropped it around her neck and tucked it under her shirt.

If Liore was right and Leander was still out there, if he did come after her, she would be ready for him.

Not knowing what to do next, she sat at her

desk, pulled out a piece of paper and began to sketch. First, she drew the large shape of a body, with a long neck and great wings. She added the features of his face and the ridges on his wings. Finally, as the sun was setting, she sketched a pool of water around him, surrounded by rocks. She added scales along the length of his body and ripples in the water.

When her mother came in to tell her that dinner was done, Morgan looked up from the drawing that she hadn't bothered trying to hide. "Can I have some colored pencils?"

"Are you back to your drawing kick again?" She stepped into the room and looked down at what Morgan was working on. "What is this?"

"It's a dragon." Morgan looked down at the partially-finished picture. "He's supposed to be green, though."

"Morgan, we talked about this. You need to focus on your school work, especially lately. Every time I come in here, you are on your video game." She looked around the room. "At least you got some of this mess cleared out. I was starting to wonder how deep it was going to get."

"I'm doing just fine in school. I just really like to draw and it gives me something to do."

Her mother just sighed. "I know you haven't been happy here. I suppose a set of pencils couldn't hurt anything." She ruffled her daughter's hair, getting her fingers caught in some of the tangles. "I think we need to go get your hair cut tomorrow." She sighed. "I just want you to promise me that you won't start to let your schoolwork slide again, OK?"

When Morgan nodded in agreement, her mother smiled. "Good. Now come downstairs and get something to eat."

After her mother left, she looked down at the picture of Stormshock. She tilted her head to the side when she realized that she had drawn him smiling, with all his sharp teeth showing. Once upon a time, that smile had scared her senseless but now she found herself smiling back at him. Maybe, wherever he was, he was still happy.

At bedtime, she snuggled down under the sheets. She rolled onto her side facing the window and closed her eyes. Immediately, she could hear a scratching noise coming from somewhere inside her walls.

Everything really had changed and Morgan had been too busy to really notice until now. With a smile, she drifted off to sleep.

Sometimes, change is a good thing.

CPSIA information can be obtained
at www.ICGtesting.com
Printed in the USA
BVHW051040171121
621846BV00012B/242